Final Payment

Pierce opened his mouth, but no words came. Every muscle in his body seemed paralyzed.

Anita slid next to him. Her eyes were dark and unreadable. Pierce watched her unbutton his Copo shirt, felt her push up the T-shirt and scratch her nails across his chest. Something peeled back; he felt a brief, sharp sting between his ribs.

She held a very small cylinder between thumb and forefinger.

"A self-destruct, Jerry."

Only one man could have ordered an involuntary implant on Jerry Pierce, and that was the man who'd given him his assignment. But it wasn't an ordinary implant, it was an agent abort. Once Pierce had completed his assignment, he was supposed to blow himself up . . .

By Crawford Kilian
Published by Ballantine Books:

The Chronoplane Wars

THE EMPIRE OF TIME
THE FALL OF THE REPUBLIC

The Empire of Time

Crawford Kilian

A Del Rey Book

BALLANTINE BOOKS • NEW YORK

A Del Rey Book
Published by Ballantine Books

Library of Congress Catalog Card Number: 78-60701

ISBN 0-345-34759-5

Manufactured in the United States of America

First Edition: December 1978
Fifth Printing: September 1987

Cover art by Stephen Hickman

For my daughters, Anna and Margaret

One:

    The intertemporal shuttle between Earth/
2015 and Beulah/1804 was an old subway train.
For decades, its three cars had carried passengers on
the old IRT line up and down Manhattan; now they
sat on a hundred-meter strip of track in a tunnel in
Flushing, on the basement level of the New York
Transferpoint Building. Twice every hour, the I-Screen
was turned on at the end of the tunnel, and the three
cars rumbled through the screen toward an identical
tunnel on Beulah. The cars were painted in Agency
blue and white, and defaced by emigrants' graffiti,
scratched, chalked, inked, and sprayed on every surface: LOIS & BILL, JAN. 27, 2015. BACKSLIDERS RULE.
AID IS NO HELP. 1804 OR BUST. The Agency for Intertemporal Development did not care; these were, after
all, the parting shots of people who would no longer be
a nuisance.

    Jerry Pierce was one of the few passengers coming
uptime on the shuttle, but over a hundred people were
waiting on the shuttle platform for the trip back. Some
were emigrants, dressed in blue-and-white Agency-is-
sue fatigues and clutching their shabby luggage. Most,
however, were Trainables on official business: civil
servants, technicians, and scholars. Some ostentatiously
wore flickreaders pushed up on their foreheads, like
sunglasses, as if their civilian clothes and attaché cases
were not enough to proclaim their privileged status.

    The shuttle came through the Screen and screeched
to a halt. Pierce was the first one off. He announced
nothing. In his dusty buckle shoes, knee breeches, and

tailcoat, he looked like a visiting endochronic—possibly a senior bureaucrat in President Jefferson's administration, traveling to the twenty-first century to beg favors from the Agency. He ignored the Trainables' patronizing smiles—and the emigrants' sullen stares—as he handed his suitcase to a porter and shot his cuff, flashing his wrist ID.

"Seventy-second floor, please. Apartment 72006."

"Yes, sir!" The porter was impressed. All apartments above the seventieth floor were reserved for top Agency staff. Pierce tipped the porter and started down the long platform to the escalators.

As he took his fifth step, time seemed to stop. Pierce's perceptions heightened and intensified, as if he had just undergone some impossible quintupling of sensory-input synthesis. He could pick out individual conversations amid the gabble and shuffle of a hundred people, but everyone was speaking so slowly that their words made no sense. A dozen different scents swirled around him. Pierce noted that exactly nine small tiles were missing from the abstract mosaic that covered the tunnel walls. He was aware of the temperature difference between his ankles and his face, and estimated it correctly at 2°C. The holoposters set into the walls blazed mindlessly at him:

WHAT ARE YOU DOING ABOUT DOOMSDAY?
THERE'S A FUTURE FOR YOU IN THE COLONIAL POLICE!
LEVY'S RYE—THE TOAST OF TWELVE CHRONOPLANES
WHAT ARE YOU DOING ABOUT DOOMSDAY?

Nothing moved.

Pierce was frightened, but observed the phenomenon with an Agent's Trained dispassion. Here was a "freeze" —an occupational hazard of Trainable Agents after years of psychoconditioning. Its onset meant the Trainable's usefulness was nearing its end.

Almost twenty years, he thought. I must be due for it. But this is just the first freeze; I could go for years without experiencing another one. I'm thirty-five; another two or three years left, anyway. An image of a cabin on the California coast, or on Thel or Ahania or even all the way back to Tharmas, flashed through his mind—a cabin with apricot and cherry trees around it: The stereotypical retirement for a used-up Agent. He would go mad with boredom. But some Agents went a whole lifetime without freezing. Wigner. Well, he's only thirty-nine, and he's got himself insulated. The bastard could spend half his time frozen solid in his office, and no one would know.

The freeze was wearing off. Down the platform, Pierce saw a young man approaching him, and worried. Had he noticed anything? The freeze could not have lasted more than a second or two; the young man could not have noticed.

Pierce recognized him at once, though they had never met. The young man was a tall, heavyset, shaggy blond and tailored denims and a white silk shirt; an agate bolo tie glinted under his short beard. He was Philon Richardson, a Trainable Climber from Los, born 985 BC in Thrace, of Dorian stock. Tested four years ago at age sixteen, and brought uptime with his equally Trainable sister for his education. Took his Trainer's family name, as did most Climbers. Under Philon's foppish appearance was still a hint of the arrogant warrior-thug he would have become if the Agency had not tapped him: a barbarian princeling, carousing in the ruins of Nestor's palace. Instead, he had become a twenty-first-century organization man—an errand boy now—but he was destined to wield more power with his fichewriter than his father ever dreamed of wielding with a sword. Still, it was interesting that anything at all was left of Philon's background. The psychoconditioners knew their job.

They greeted each other with a nod. Accustomed to high-speed data acquisition through the flickreader, Trainables found normal speech tedious; among themselves they spoke elliptically, or else imbued normal speech with irony and ambiguity. On this occasion, as relative strangers surrounded by a crowd of unTrainables, courtesy dictated the latter form of speech.

"Good morning, Mr. Pierce. Welcome home."

"Good morning, Philon. Thank you; it's good to be back."

They strolled through the crowd to the escalators. The only lingering effect of the freeze, so far as Pierce could tell, was a slight euphoria.

"Wigner must be eager to see me."

"Very eager, Mr. Pierce."

"Too bad. I was hoping to catch up on my sleep before reporting in."

Philon smiled sympathetically and made amiable small talk: the clammy New York winter weather, the latest Agency gossip, the nasty new flu virus that had slipped in from one of the Paleolithic chronoplanes and taken 150,000 lives in the past month, mostly in the slums of Rio, São Paulo, and Asunción. Pierce said little, nodding absently.

They ascended the escalator to the Transferpoint Concourse, a circular roofed plaza 250 meters in diameter. The main exit led outside to New York, Earth/2015. The other exits, spaced around the plaza's circumference and marked by glowing holoposters, led to:

New-York, Beulah/1804;
Vikingshaven, Eden/1180;
Port Palisades, Ahania/107;
Chronoport, Los/965 BC;
Ishizawa City, Albion/8127 BC;
Glaciopolis, Orc/12,165 BC;
Simpsonville, Luvah/22,233 BC;
Johnson Station, Urthona/26,991 BC;
Hudson Valley, Vala 34,468 BC;
Welcome, Thel/47,114 BC;
Lindsay City, Tharmas/70,787 BC.

There were, of course, no shuttles to Ulro/2239 or Urizen/3571. The dead worlds uptime were visited only through special I-Screens by highly trained scavengers who darted into the ruined cities seeking clues to the nature of Doomsday.

Thousands poured through the Concourse. Philon and Pierce ignored them as they headed for the elevators to the upper floors of the Transferpoint Building. They stepped alone into the VIP elevator, and Philon inserted a key into the control panel. He pressed 112: Operations Division, Wigner's floor. The doors sighed shut, and Pierce sank into one of the easy chairs, stretching his long legs. He smiled tiredly at Philon, who smiled back and remained standing.

"You're new with the Agency, aren't you?"

"That's right, sir. I've been with the Director's Office about a month now. It's a good place to work."

"And how long have you been on Earth?"

Philon's smile faded a little. To continue normal speech in private was proper enough between one of Pierce's rank and one of Philon's, but it was rude to ask about what should already be known.

"Three years. My sister and I were Tested in '06 and brought uptime in '07. She's interning now in a hospital in Montevideo. As I suppose you know." He had spelled it all out—a counterinsult.

"How does she like it? Better than being the property of some asshole in a bronze jockstrap, hey?"

Philon watched the floor numbers flashing above the door. "Hmm," he replied. He did not like having his endochronic background thrown in his face. Such rudeness was to be expected from Backsliders, un-Trainables who were being crowded off Earth to make room for Climbers like himself, but for a Senior Field Agent to talk this way was too much.

Pierce was wryly aware of the reasons for his deliberate discourtesy. Philon reminded him of himself at twenty: an apprentice hatchetman, pleasantly aware of his elite status but not yet experienced enough to begin to doubt the value of his job. Something else about the young Dorian also bothered him, but he couldn't identify it. A slight kinesic tension, a glint of hostility in the respectful smile. He had seen it many times, usually in men preparing to try to kill him. But in Philon such tension made no sense. Let it pass: an aftereffect, no doubt, of the freeze.

The door opened, and Pierce stood up.

"After you, Philon."

"That's all right, I'm going on up to one twenty-one. Glad to have met you, Mr. Pierce. I hope we'll meet again soon." Pierce waved a vague good-bye, and walked into Wigner's outer office. For some reason, he did not entirely relax until the elevator doors had closed behind him.

Floor 112 had for Pierce a pleasant air of lived-in luxury: good teak tables with coffee rings marring their elegant surfaces; some early Booth cartoons, originals, tacked on official bulletin boards; thick Danish carpets a bit overdue for cleaning. Two dozen clerks, men and women, were running floods of data through the flickertube terminals evenly spaced around the large main office. The meter-square screens shimmered with a dozen colors, like high-speed kaleidoscopes. The clerks were dressed in overalls, chitons, jeans, brocade robes; their only common denominators seemed to be youth and a passion for houseplants, which adorned the terminals like ivy on gravestones.

Holograms glowed on most walls and partitions: second-century Rome from the air; the scrub forests of the Dogger Plain, where the Thames and Rhine merged and flowed north to the Norwegian Bight on Tharmas; a twelfth-century Buddhist monk in Kyoto, all jolliness and wrinkles; a Paleo-Indian band celebrating a good hunt in an Albionese Arizona swamp. The pictures had all been taken by the staff of Floor 112, while vacationing; working Field Agents had no time for travelogue holography.

There were no windows on Floor 112. The Operations Division was interested only in the worlds downtime whose affairs it guided, and in the worlds uptime whose fate it sought to escape.

Pierce walked up to Judy Willems, Wigner's staff coordinator.

"Married yet?" A running gag between them, and all the greeting he needed to give her.

"Not yet." A dazzling smile. She was twenty-four and very good-looking. No lipstick or breast powder —she needed no cosmetics—and her dark tan and thick yellow hair were nicely set off by her warm-gold sarong. "Pooped?"

"*Mph.*"

"Dinner tonight?"

"My place or yours?" Another running gag.

"Mine. The squalor you live in makes me want to wash dishes and scrub floors."

"Atavist! When?"

"Oh—1930ish."

"Why not earlier?"

"You won't be through until 1800; you have an all-day appointment with Dr. Suad."

"Oh boy. How can Wigner send me out again when I've just got back? What's up?"

She shrugged. "Something to do with Colonials. I don't know the details." He could tell, though, that she knew enough to make her nervous.

"Christ. Rather deal with endos." He shrugged too. "Tell him I'm here."

Eric Wigner's office, at first glance, could have belonged to an Agency Librarian (Grade 6). It was windowless, rather small, and cluttered with computer cartridges, microfiche cards, and the inevitable houseplants; Wigner seemed to be particularly fond of piggyback plants, grape ivy, and maidenhair fern. Then one noticed his century-old rolltop desk, the shelves filled with genuine hardcover books (including a first edition of *1984*), the battered couch covered with real leather, and realized that one was indeed dealing with the Agency's Permanent Deputy for Operations, a man who could found or topple empires, and often did.

Pierce walked in, kicked off his shoes, and collapsed on the couch. "What is this shit?"

Wigner tilted back in his swivel chair and put his

slippered feet up on the desk. He grinned through his bushy gray mustache. He was a middle-sized man, bald, pink-cheeked, and physically unimpressive. Pierce was some fifteen centimeters taller, and had the physique of a racing-shell oarsman, but there was no question who was boss.

"It's always the same shit," Wigner replied. He chose normal speech, and even inflated it slightly. "When I heard about this problem, Jerry, I asked myself: Who among my many fine Senior Field Agents has the brains, the guts, the determination for this arduous and demanding assignment? Those were my exact words. And of course the answer was you."

"How so?"

"In a minute. Tell me about Brother Thomas."

Pierce pulled a cassette from his breast pocket and scaled it across the office. Wigner caught it with startling quickness.

"All on tape. The meeting went pretty well. Domestic politics: he wanted to switch some Agency funds from medicare to highways and transport. A lot of his people are unhappy about equal medical treatment for Black and Indian kids. They *really* resent it when Testing time comes and we take just as many Blacks and Indians as whites—"

"Some of whom will later come back to Beulah as Trained administrators."

"They *do* hate to see those Blacks using flickreaders and telling 'em not to pee in the soup."

"You brought Jefferson around?"

"Not really sure. The money stays in medicare, but we agreed—I agreed—to ease up on our antislavery campaign. That may have been just what he was after in the first place. Very complicated man, Mr. Jefferson. Pity we couldn't have Tested him in his teens. Never saw a more obvious wasted Trainable."

Wigner shrugged. "They can maintain slavery as long as they like, for all I care. Just so they sell us the Trainable slaves at age sixteen." He snorted. "The only reason we bitch about slavery is because people here on Earth expect us to. Domestic politics."

Pierce noticed a new snapshot on Wigner's desk and sat up for a closer look. It was a cheap Polaroid 3-D photo, not a real hologram, that showed Wigner and Napoleon Bonaparte sitting at a little table in a formal garden. Both men were squinting amiably into the sun, and the photographer's shadow had fallen across the table.

"When was *that* taken?"

"Yesterday," Wigner replied innocently.

"On Beulah without informing me?"

"Well—you were busy with Jefferson, and something came up—I just popped back for the weekend. Yes, I should've notified you."

"What's Boney want now?"

"We're helping him raid London next month. He wants a freer hand."

"I thought the Brits were coming round."

"Some are. Cabinet's split. Boney's raid should bring Pitt down. But he wants to establish a proper beachhead and take over."

"Does he, now?"

"Endos are like babies—testing, testing. We'll stage the raid our way, and in return we get complete control of the French schools—"

"And the Brits will finally allow us to Test their kids."

"Mm. Think of the valuable personnel we've lost through their pigheadedness."

"From Pitt's point of view, we'll do to them what they did to the Scots—co-opt their best people and turn the whole country to our purposes."

"You're too fair. A blind man *has* no point of view." Wigner gestured to the hologram on the wall behind him. "Pitt's seen that picture, but he doesn't understand that it makes his petty nationalism pointless."

The hologram, a meter on a side, was a view of Ulro taken by a drone space probe. The continents—North America, Europe, part of Africa—were pinkish-brown and sharply outlined against the dirty gray of the empty ocean basins. Everything looked very clear, because there was almost no atmosphere on the Earth of the twenty-third century. In the hologram, noon was about on the meridian of London. In its ruined streets, the temperature would be close to 100°C. A thin, fierce CO_2 wind would be hissing over the fused rubble. Pierce knew what it was like in that London; he had been there once, and elsewhere on Ulro four other times.

Wigner, meditating, filled his pipe and lit it.

"Sometimes," he finally said, "I think the historic chronoplanes are more trouble than they're worth. Too stable, too backward—nothing but raw materials and Trainable manpower. Can't even colonize much—start getting endo revolts . . . Imagine a chronoplane between 1920, 1950? Get Fermi and Oppenheimer working on the Doomsday problem."

Pierce laughed briefly. "If they were Trainable."

Wigner grinned around his pipe. "Levelheaded Jerry!"

"What's all this Colonial business?"

"You've talked to Judy. Mm. When were you last on Orc?"

"Two years ago—as you should know. That Secessionist mob in the Colonial Police. Routine."

"Let's hope this is too. The Commissioner there—Gersen—has sent me a report on suspected sabotage at the Weapons Development Site. He wants us to check it out."

"Sabotage the WDS? Who? Culties?"

"Nobody colonizes Orc unless they're screened-out loyals."

"Knotholers—any illegal I-Screens detected?"

Wigner shook his head. "Probably just poor administration. Or—"

"Domestic politics."

"Yup. After all, unTrainables administering Trainables . . ." Wigner looked sour. Pierce nodded; it was an old irritation. Colonies were governed by and for unTrainables. The WDS was too vulnerable, and too dangerous, to be placed on Earth. Problems were inevitable.

Wigner picked up a microfiche in a pink Top Secret envelope and handed it to Pierce. "Take a look; tell me what you think."

Pierce inserted the 3x10cm microfiche in his flickreader and switched it on. The fifty-five-page memorandum took him less than thirty seconds to read and assimilate. He gave it back to Wigner, who dropped the microfiche in his desktop shredder.

"Well, well," said Pierce.

"Mm. Go take some Briefing and Conditioning and head downtime to Orc in the morning."

"Now look, Eric. I deserve a rest after six weeks among the rednecks. Is the situation that urgent?"

"It is."

"Why?"

"Now, come on, Jerry." Wigner spoke in the soft murmur his subordinates knew well. His words had a certain rote quality; he had repeated this often. "Doomsday is still on schedule, just seventy-four years away. We still don't know what will cause it. If it turns out to be an alien attack, Earth must be able to defend itself."

"I don't need the whole sermon."

"Of course not." They both knew that Pierce's conditioning had been reinforced by Wigner's cueing. That conditioning would make him miserable if he remained on Earth for even an extra day.

"Is it too early for a drink?" Pierce asked.

"Ah. Gives me an excuse to show off the Napoleon brandy I brought back."

"Nice change from Tom Jefferson's white lightning."

Sitting in the small, disordered office surrounded by houseplants, the two men sipped brandy from styrofoam cups. "Well, it's not *bad*," said Wigner, "but it's certainly not all it's cracked up to be."

"Give it another century."

"Let's discuss your trip. If you catch the first jet tomorrow from Kennedy—"

Pierce shook his head. "I'd rather shuttle back from here to Glaciopolis, and fly across to Farallon City."

"Waste of time. There's only one transcontinental flight a day on Orc. Even with the best connections, you'll have a three-hour wait at the Glaciopolis airport."

"Doesn't matter. It'll let me see what sort of changes the Colonials are making. From Farallon City I can take the noon flight to Los Alamitos."

Wigner shrugged. "Suit yourself. I'll have Gersen's staff advised, and you can meet him in Farallon before you fly down."

"Good. I assume this is not a covert investigation."

"No. It's a small world at Los Alamitos. Any new face is sure to attract attention. You could fake it fairly well as a scientist, of course, at least for a few days. But the cover would keep you pinned down to one project. So just be your normal inquisitive self, and see everything." He stood up, ending the interview. "Break a leg, Jerry."

"Thanks, Eric." They shook hands; Wigner held on a moment longer than he needed to. Pierce felt a small glow of affection. Wigner liked most people only as they were useful to him and to the Agency. It was somehow touching to find a hint of personal fondness coming through.

Back at Judy's desk, Pierce found his documents already prepared: a new Senior Official's visa for his intertemporal passport, an Agency credit card, and part of his medical papers.

"You get the rest of Medical Doc when you finish B&C," she told him. "New routine."

"Fine. Is Dr. Suad ready for me?"

She whispered into her ringmike, then looked into space for a moment as the answer whispered back through the receiver hidden in her ear. "All set. Have a good session. See you tonight."

They gave each other a friendly kiss, and Pierce

headed for the elevator. On Floor 130, he stepped into a very different atmosphere. It looked something like a doctor's waiting room, circa 1955 U.S., complete with contemporary magazines: *Life, The Saturday Evening Post,* a *Collier's* special issue describing a Third World War that never happened. Suad enjoyed collecting such things, and on his Agency salary he could afford to.

The nurse-receptionist, however, clashed with the decor. He was a burly young man in hospital-green linen blouse and brown corduroy slacks. He sat behind a little sliding window, flickreading. Pierce reached silently through the window and picked up the microfiche envelope. It displayed a glossy, lurid photo of two gladiators disemboweling each other in the Colosseum, under the title *Blood-Slaves of Caesar,* by Proculus Gratianus as told to Bert Schwartz.

Pierce laughed. "Shame on you, reading this crap." The nurse whipped off the flickreader and grinned sheepishly.

"Oh, uh, hi, Mr. Pierce."

"Lost in a fog of carnography." Pierce shook his head in mock horror. "Isn't there enough perversion in these old magazines your boss is so fond of?"

"Those? Never even look at 'em."

"Is that so?"

"They're—you know—unTrainable media."

"Ah."

The nurse had already pushed a button on his desk intercom, and Dr. Suad appeared quietly through a side door. He was stocky, with coarse black hair to his shoulders and heavy, cleanshaven jowls—an affectation now that beards were fashionable. Pierce wished he had his whiskers again; they had been sacrificed in deference to the style of Jefferson's era, which was self-consciously rigid about resisting twenty-first-century fashions.

"Hello, Mr. Pierce. How do you do, sir?" A firm, dry handshake. "How are we today?" Always formal, as befitted a B&C man; flippancy in a brainwasher would be intolerable.

"Dr. Suad. I am very well, thank you." Pierce had very nearly blanked out his memory of the freeze, and no hint of dishonesty appeared in his voice. He offered Dr. Suad a slight tilt of the head, for even Senior Field Agents must defer to this man and his colleagues. "I believe we have a great deal to do today."

"Yes."

"Well, let's get on with it."

"Of course." Suad invited him into the darkened room behind. It was furnished sparely: a narrow water bed covered with an institutional-blue sheet; a light Finnish armchair; a teak cabinet and matching wardrobe. Three walls were painted flat white; on the fourth, behind the head of the bed, was a computer terminal.

"Please make yourself comfortable, Mr. Pierce."

Pierce stripped off his clothes and hung them in the wardrobe. For almost three minutes he sat on the edge of the bed, hyperventilating. Meanwhile, Suad punched a code on the computer keyboard; it replied at once by slapping a sheaf of microfiche cards into the hardcopy hopper.

Pierce stretched out on the bed, his body seeming gaunt in the dimness. He had removed his wig, revealing a short mat of brown-black hair on a long, narrow skull.

Saud ignored him for the moment. He wore a flickreader, and fed microfiche cards into it with the same impassive efficiency his nurse had used in devouring *Blood-Slaves of Caesar*. After the machine had devoured the last card, he removed his flickreader and took a hypospray pistol from the teak cabinet. He loaded it with six cartridges and pressed its flat muzzle against Pierce's arm.

"Yes, a long session, Mr. Pierce."

Pierce said nothing. Suad lowered a flickertube over Pierce's face; the tube would transmit data directly from the computer.

"Count to ten, please."

"One . . . two . . . three . . ." Pierce was out.

Briefing required suspension of consciousness. This was high-speed Training, and a conscious mind would only impede the process. What would take seven or eight days to absorb by flickreading—or two or three years for an unTrainable to read and comprehend—Pierce would learn in four hours. The flickertube was focused on the inside of his eye, and transmitted information as fast as the optic nerve could carry it. Since Suad had given him 100 ccs of buffered nikethamide, that was very fast indeed. The spectrum of RNA catalysts which preceded the nerve stimulant would ensure that each datum was recorded in retrievable form.

The flickertube went on, but from Suad's point of view nothing could be seen but a rapidly shifting blur of colors around Pierce's eyes: green, yellow, red, purple, green, red, blue, green. Every time Pierce blinked, the tube cut out for an instant.

Unhurriedly, Suad taped electrodes to Pierce's temples, throat, wrists, and ankles. He hummed tunelessly as a readout bank came to life on the computer wall, quantifying Pierce's physiological status. The computer flashed a long prescription, and a few seconds later a small plastic box glided out of a chute and onto a shelf in the cabinet. Suad opened the box, withdrew the fifteen cartridges it contained, and loaded them into his pistol. He began to inject them in carefully timed sequence, keeping constant watch on the computer dials that recorded the changes induced by the drugs. He saw nothing unexpected or untoward.

An hour passed. Suad sprayed solvent on a small area beneath Pierce's left nipple. A patch of what looked like skin suddenly dissolved, revealing a plastic ring, three centimeters in diameter, embedded between two ribs. Suad peered into the ring with a modified otoscope. The ring was the mouth of a cylinder, seven and a half centimeters long, sealed at the other end. Suad inserted a smaller version of a regular hypospray cartridge into the cylinder, where it fit very snugly. Another spray; the ring was once again hidden under a pseudoderm patch.

Still humming, Suad left the room. He slouched into an easy chair in the waiting room and picked up one of his beloved old magazines, a *Galaxy* from the early '50's. The cover and pages had been preserved with a compound related to pseudoderm.

"Pretty slow afternoon," his nurse remarked.

"Mm-hm."

Two other Agents came in for B&C during the afternoon, but they were relatively routine jobs, finished before Pierce was even half through. When Pierce did begin to stir, Suad was waiting beside his bed. There was one last injection, a mild tranquilizer. Suad removed the electrodes, swung the flickertube back into the computer wall, and waited.

"Four . . . five . . ." Pierce blinked awake. He sighed, then sat up and swung his feet to the floor. He snorted, coughed, scratched at the sticky patch an electrode had left on one wrist.

"Everything all right?" he asked.

"Mm-hm. You're not an Alpha-class Trainable for nothing, Mr. Pierce. There might be, mm, three other people in the whole Agency who can equal you for receptivity to B&C."

Suad deliberately fumbled with the hypospray pistol, letting it slip from his fingers. Pierce moved off the bed like a striking snake, and caught the pistol before it had fallen half a meter.

"Hyped reflexes," Pierce remarked casually, handing back the pistol.

Suad nodded. "Grade Twelve reflexes and tripled sensory-input synthesis."

Pierce strode to the wardrobe and slid open the door, just a little too hard.

"Why?"

"I couldn't say, Mr. Pierce. I just fill prescriptions."

"Have *you* ever had hyped reflexes, Dr. Suad?"

"Of course. In med school. Grade Four, for a few hours."

Pierce smiled wryly as he pulled on his stockings and knee breeches. He gave Suad a half-second's eye contact, reminding him of what they both knew: Pierce was a natural Grade 4.

"Well, Dr. Suad, on some slow afternoon you ought to ask your nurse to hype you up to Nine or Ten." He yanked his shirt on, and tied the stock with irritable, abrupt gestures. "It's miserable. You're always hungry, but food tastes—metallic. Sometimes there's a hell of a ringing in your ears. You fidget all the time."

"Mm-hm. Well, remember to do your breathing exercises; they should help reduce the fidgeting."

He ushered Pierce into the waiting room. It was empty; the nurse had gone home. Saud and Pierce shook hands, a little relieved to be out of each other's company; then Pierce took the elevator down to his residential floor.

Why Grade 12? And why the tripled SIS? Pierce was sourly aware that B&C had put him in a condition closely resembling this morning's freeze: everything had once more become painfully sharp and clear. Vision, hearing, smell, taste, touch (heat, pressure, texture), balance—all were focused uncomfortably tightly, and it would take time to adapt. When his tripled SIS was eventually cleared, the world would again seem drab and insubstantial until he had adapted. His sense of smell seemed especially sharp: he could detect six different perfume residues in the elevator, mixed with the characteristic body odors of perhaps ten or twelve men and as many women. There was a whiff of marijuana, and a trace of flatulence.

You don't get Grade 12 and tripled SIS unless you need them, he reflected. (Would the elevator *never* reach his floor?) Wigner must be expecting trouble. What kind of trouble could there be?

A stroboscopic memory of the last time he'd had Grade 12, a good five years earlier: a winter night in Gaul, on Ahania, with snow thick on the ground. The tent of an obstreperous Roman general, four guards outside dying swiftly and silently, the snow squeaking a little as they fall into it. Inside the tent, the general quick enough to reach for his gun but dead before his

fingers can close around the butt; his boy lover, too terrified to shriek, peeping out of the blankets still warm
from the general's body. He gasps as Pierce turns the
pistol toward him and the flechettes strike.

What the hell kind of trouble could there be? He reviewed his Briefing, or started to, as the elevator door
finally slid open on his floor.

—*I've been blocked.* He fumbled for his door key,
let himself in, and stripped off his clothes. Why blocked?
Maybe Judy would know.

He felt a bit shaky. Blocked Briefing; tripled SIS;
Grade 12. Pierce shivered with the chill of fear, mixed
pleasantly with anticipation. I'm too old for this Special
Operations commando crap—Christ, thirty-five, had
my first freeze, I'm no kid any more. But *they* don't
think I'm too old, and the adrenalin trip is as sweet as
ever and sure to improve, because I've been loaded
and cocked and I'm going to Orc to zap a bad guy. He
remembered the euphoria he'd felt in Gaul stealing
through the snowbound camp to the tent with the eagerness of the trysting lover.

Breathing exercises. He stood naked in the middle of
his modestly furnished living room, breathing in a
rhythm designed to metabolize the adrenalin, relax the
muscles. After a minute or two he calmed down,
laughed aloud at himself, and headed for the shower.

Two:

Pierce's earliest memories were of the mid-'80s, when he was three or four. The Piggly Wiggly supermarket in Taos: its high windows cracked and boarded over, the parking lot full of squatters' tents and squatters' trash; the broad stumps of the cottonwoods that once screened the lot from the road. He would clamber up on a stump, run recklessly around the edge, and then run on to the next one, until his mother lost patience and dragged him into the lot and through the doors that no longer opened automatically. The aisles were interestingly dirty, the half-empty shelves spooky in the dim light. Market guards, usually Anglos, wore holstered revolvers and carried handcuffs at their belts; one of the guards once gave him a stick of gum. His mother's ration book had a green plastic cover, dull and cracked, with interesting stamps inside: blue ones with an eagle on them, green ones with a smiling man, red ones with a rocket.

Those were very early memories, from the first austerity years. Another memory, a painful one, from the late '80s: coming home from the Piggly Wiggly—now Federal Foodstuffs Dispensary 1207—with his mother. Each of them carried a small shopping bag with the week's rations—flour, synthetic sugar, soy bacon, cabbage—and in his bag was a special treat, a chocolate bar his mother had paid three stamps for. A gang of Hispano kids, just a couple of years older than Jerry, jumped them, snatched the shopping bags, and sprinted off. One of the boys was Pete Gomez, who lived in the condominium next door. He was big for his age, and he knocked Jerry's mother off her feet.

"Jerry, are you all right?" his mother asked shakily as she pulled herself up. Her skirt was torn at the hem.

"Yeah. But they took my chocolate bar. I want my chocolate bar, Ma."

"And I want my groceries, goddamn it."

But Mrs. Gomez denied everything, screamed at them, threatened. Pete wasn't around at all the rest of the day. Next morning, Pete told Jerry they'd eaten the chocolate and bacon, and scattered the rest around an empty lot.

"Dumb bastard," sneered Ramiro Espinosa, who was thirteen or fourteen. "Coulda sold that stuff for plenty."

The next week they were ambushed again. Jerry tried to fight, but Pete knocked him flat. This time, his mother cried; they had no more stamps until the end of the month.

In 1990, the Ethnic Integrity Act imposed de jure residential segregation, and the Chavez family had to move into an all-Hispano district. Jerry's mother married a police sergeant, and things improved. But one night in 1992, his stepfather was run off the road near Arroyo Hondo. He died a week later. After that they lived on a pension, while Jerry grew up enough to enter high school and begin worrying about the draft. The Venezuelan war was technically over, but a thousand Americans a month were still dying in the Pacification Zones. American "consultants" in Canada were being sniped at. The Polish revolt was still on, threatening to spread into a general European war.

"Why not take this new Trainability test?" his high-school counselor suggested as Jerry neared sixteen. Looks like a pretty promising field. If you've got the talent for it, you're sure to get a commission in the service. Sure beats foot-slogging." To Jerry, who was big, healthy, and athletic, it sounded good.

Training was only a few years old then, a half-understood technique that enabled those with the talent to absorb and retain incredible amounts of information in a very short time. Only about one person in six or seven had potential Trainability, though, and Testing wasn't yet mandatory. Trainables had to be spotted in midadolescence, when the talent matured, and Training had to begin almost at once. Those who postponed it for more than a year or two usually lost the ability; the best they could get from Training was higher reading speed.

But Trainables had already made enough of an impact on society to be unpopular. A seventeen-year-old Trainable and a desktop computer could process as much information in a day as a whole platoon of un-Trainable clerks could manage in a month. One precocious fifteen-year-old girl, starting with five-hundred dollars borrowed from her father, had taken just two years to make six million dollars in the commodities market. A nineteen-year-old Italian—one of the first to acquire a medical degree through Training—had spent a mere six months absorbing the entire world literature on cancer research and was then able to isolate twelve separate cancer-triggering mechanisms and identify the means for neutralizing ten of them. A year later, brushing up on the literature inspired by his own findings, he found the neutralizers for the remaining two.

These were not universally admired achievements in a world already overpopulated and on the edge of economic collapse. But the Trainables seemed unstoppable. Most of them found immediate work in administering the vast, rickety social structures that sheltered the rest of mankind. Their sheer knowledge kept the food growing, the trains running, the turbines spinning. Even the worldwide antiTrainable riots of '92 failed to stop the takeover. Wars were endemic all over the planet; famine had become permanent in South America, Africa, India, and Indonesia. Over 6.2 billion people, half of them under twenty-five, were struggling for bare subsistence. "It is us or catastrophe," a Trainable French diplomat warned the UN in 1995.

A year after passing his Trainability test—with an Alpha-18, one of the highest scores ever recorded in the United States—Jerry became a (T)-Colonel in the U. S. Army. He held the equivalents of four master's degrees, and was working on three Ph.D.s. Thanks to the Civil Emergency Act of 1995, his powers far exceeded those normal for his rank. The Continental Army Command was the chief arm of government in most areas of the United States, and Jerry found himself, at age seventeen, the de facto dictator of eastern Oregon and all of Idaho.

He had no illusions, however, about his probable future. "It is us *and* catastrophe," he often said to himself. The system was breaking down, and only a Trainable could really know how swift the process was. In a year, or two, or five, the real die-off would hit. He took an adolescent's glum relish in private debates with fellow Trainables: would it be a nuclear war, with an inevitable attendant destruction of the ozone layer? A wild mutant virus, natural or man-made, spreading unstoppably through the world's undernourished billions? A poisoning of the seas? A blend of all these?

He carried out his job with the impersonal pleasure of a skilled craftsman and viewed his successes with ironic detachment. Why, after all, seek to preserve the lives of the doomed? Why shoot the robber who must die soon in any case? He could moralize as well as anyone, but under all the cant about law and order and making the system work he recognized in himself only one real motive: personal stubbornness. He would shoot looters and jail refugees because he had the power to do so, and the will. He would protect his people because doing so was a challenge, a test of his new skills. He liked the work, but knew it couldn't last.

Of course, he as well as everyone else was taken completely by surprise when the crisis ended in the fall of 1998 with the accidental discovery of an emergency exit for all mankind.

That October, a graduate physics student named Richard Ishizawa—one of the last unTrainables in the

United States to be granted a Ph.D.—set up a novel hypermagnetic array in Cave 9 of the Fermi Accelerator Laboratory in Batavia, Illinois. It should have created a field capable of deflecting an extremely high-energy particle beam in any desired direction with very little energy loss. Ishizawa hoped to produce a focused beam of unprecedented intensity with which quarks might be flushed out of the subatomic underbrush more easily than earlier techniques permitted.

His experiment should have worked perfectly, as was later determined by very hard detective work, on the future chronoplanes of Ulro and Urizen, Ishizawa had indeed produced his field and found his quarks. He later died in a food riot in 2007, during the last convulsions of the old social order.

On Earth, however, a microcircuit failed, as Ishizawa himself discovered very quickly. As a result of that failure, a very different field was created, and the vacuum in Cave 9 abruptly filled with air, leaf debris, and soil particles. Ishizawa had opened the first I-Screen, and the TV monitor in Cave 9 gave him a fine view of an eighteenth-century Illinois forest.

Every other project at Fermi lab stopped dead. A security cloak fell over the Laboratory, and urgent, discreet calls went out to other physicists, to chemists, botanists, astronomers, and anthropologists. Cautiously, they followed Ishizawa through the Screen into what was first called a "topological singularity," then a "temporal incongruity." A lover of the poetry of William Blake, Ishizawa called his new world Beulah—and was astonished when Beulah turned out to be Earth in the summer of 1787, when Blake was still very much alive.

A kind of hysteria struck the Fermi lab scientists and spread to the government—then to other governments. Pierce learned of the discovery in November, when most Trainables did, and he kept close track of developments. This was easy, since most Trainables had already lost their loyalties to national authorities and routinely informed one another of important events their governments were trying to keep secret.

By Christmas, I-Screen theory was well advanced, but it was not to progress much further for a generation. The theory was simple, but its implications had literally changed history. At the point of the initial big bang, cosmologists speculated, every particle in the universe had undergone singular forces so intense that it had oscillated in time. A single cosmos transformed itself into a series, each cosmos virtually identical except for its chronoplane, or location on the time line.

Ishizawa's major contribution to this theory was to predict the "Heisenberg cascade"—the effect of subatomic particles' being in different places or carrying different energies, on different chronoplanes. In a few cases, a cascade would produce detectable differences between chronoplanes. There might, Ishizawa speculated, be species on Beulah that were unknown to Earth. Furthermore, persons important in the history of Earth might never have lived on Beulah. Ishizawa did not know, and never lived to learn, that his failed microcircuit itself resulted from just such a Heisenberg cascade.

His theory also predicted that proper modulation of the I-Screen would reveal other chronoplanes. Such modulations, on a trial-and-error basis, were carried out. But most tests produced nothing but the kind of field Ishizawa had been trying to produce in the first place. Gradually, however, other chronoplanes were located—twelve altogether, falling at more and more widely scattered points in the past. Each was given a name from Blake's poetic mythology.

However, Ishizawa never lived to see them all. While several teams were probing the past, he sought the future. After a six-week search, he died discovering Ulro, then at 2215 AD. The I-Screen was operating in an ordinary lab when it opened on Ulro, and the vacuum on the other side imploded the whole room. Before the array collapsed, killing the Screen, enough radiation came through to contaminate the whole building. But a shielded VTR tape was retrieved, giving Earth its first glimpse of Doomsday: the ruins of what was clearly the Fermi Accelerator Laboratory, blazing under the Sun in a black, airless sky.

Four months of secret preparation went into the next probe to Ulro, at the end of which a robot tank was finally sent through. After a four-day round trip to Evanston, the tank returned to the Batavia ruins and fired a canister of tapes and photos through the I-Screen. The vehicle itself was too radioactive to return.

Scientists now entered the field of genuine futurology and tried to determine, from evidence as ambiguous as an oracle's warning, just what was going to happen to cause that cataclysm. Once the manned tank probes ventured into the future, they learned a few things very quickly.

Doomsday had occurred on April 22, 2089. Something had struck a world with a population of only three billion, most of whom were Trainables. They were living in a world commonwealth of peaceful but regimented societies that had emerged, after the turn of the millennium, from the wreckage of the unTrainable order. These societies were technically far ahead of the 1990s, and the broken bits of their technologies were as tantalizing and mysterious as a cassette tape would have been to Leonardo da Vinci.

But the people of Ulro without doubt had been ignorant of the I-Screen, and of the existence of the chronoplanes. This crucial fact offered Earth at least a fighting chance of avoiding Ulro's fate.

So I-Screens were secretly set up elsewhere on Earth and they opened onto Ulro—and, a little later, onto Urizen in the late thirty-third century. At a high cost in lives and equipment, the nature of the cataclysm became clearer.

On Doomsday, an intense beam of energy more than three-thousand kilometers in diameter had struck the planet's dayside at the equator off the west coast of

South America and then traveled west across the Pacific. The beam had probably remained stationary, while the planet rotated beneath it. The ocean had been vaporized under that beam, and a gigantic flower of superheated steam and pulverized rock had risen a thousand kilometers before it blossomed in space. As the beam traveled, the flower became a curtain, a wall of vaporized water, soil, and stone that followed the beam around the planet and gradually drifted into space in what must have been a gloriously beautiful white spiral. No one would have lived long enough to see it, however. All life on the surface must have perished within hours of the beam's first impact, for the shock wave it generated smashed and buried virtually everything on the planet under an atmospheric tsunami of debris.

The beam traveled seventeen times around the world before abruptly and inexplicably disappearing. By that time the entire atmosphere and all surface water had been blown into space. Somehow the Van Allen Belt had vanished, allowing a steady downpour of ionizing radiation to reach the surface. Violent earthquakes and volcanic eruptions had broken out everywhere as the crust rebounded under the dead ocean floors. The vast, irregular trench cut by the beam soon filled with magma, like blood clotting in a wound. Meteorites, most of them quite small, began to lunarize the dead planet.

On Urizen, over a thousand years after Doomsday, volcanic outgasing had begun to replace the lost atmosphere with a tenuous envelope of CO_2 and water vapor. In the polar regions, there was enough winter precipitation to sustain a few colonies of tough lichens whose spores had somehow survived. In a million centuries, life might arise again in the Earth's shallow new seas—or it might not.

Telescopes set up on Ulro and Urizen revealed the existence of a dead colony on the Moon, and documents indicated that on Doomsday a manned base had also existed on Mars, but these outposts had evidently not long survived. Manned space probes might have been sent out, but were not. Too much evidence existed to suggest that Doomsday had been caused by alien intruders, who might still be in the neighborhood. Attracting their attention might lead to their discovery of the downtime chronoplanes.

Other Doomsday theories postulated less sinister mechanisms: collision with an antimatter planetoid, a "macroflare" ejected from the sun or a scientific experiment gone hideously wrong. Each had its exponents, but nothing was certain except that on two chronoplanes, life had been expunged on April 22, 2089.

Of necessity secrecy was finally dropped altogether. What had been discovered was brought before the moribund United Nations, and in less than a year the UN had dissolved itself and the International Federation had been established in its place. As the first world government, the IF held extraordinary powers; not only did it rule the nations of Earth, it extended its power into the other chronoplanes. The IF held one purpose paramount: discovering the nature of Doomsday and, if possible preventing its occurring on Earth and the downtime chronoplanes. If Doomsday were found to be inevitable, the IF would carry out the evacuation of Earth and, eventually, the other chronoplanes in an organized retreat.

This overriding mission guided all IF policy. Elite teams, more idolized than the old astronauts ever were, made scavenge jumps into the future, bringing back the shattered toys and tools of their great-grandchildren. Gigantic scientific efforts were launched to force-grow a technology equal or superior to that of the next century. As a result, there was an instant shortage of useful labor. Trainability Testing became mandatory for every adolescent on Earth, and teams began to ransack the downtime worlds for Trainables among the endochronics. At the same time, Earth's hungry un-

Trainables began to pour into the sparsely populated worlds of the past, building new cities, plowing virgin soil, drilling for oil and digging for minerals to sustain the garrison world that Earth was fast becoming.

Pierce quickly became involved. The Agency for Intertemporal Development was one of the IF's first creations, and it needed plenty of Trainables. His first assignment was in late '99 as chief of a Testing and Recruitment team in the Caucasus on Luvah, where they ambushed Paleolithic tribes with tranquilizing darts, Tested the adolescents, and carried off those with Trainability. It was hard work, because the first scouts on Luvah—as on other chronoplanes—had accidentally spread a variety of twentieth century viruses that wiped out sixty percent of Luvah's endos in less than three years. Pierce's T&R team found more corpses than live bodies in the caves and campsites they prowled.

Those, of course, had been the bad old days, when Earth was still learning to cope with its new discoveries and millions died because of ignorance or accident. But with AID's growing expertise, Earth had come through the first decade fairly well; almost two billion emigrants had colonized the past, and millions more were going through the I-Screens every day. They fished the teeming glacial seas of Vala and Thel; logged the endless redwood forests of Luvah and Urthona; grazed a million head of cattle on the Sahara grasslands of Albion and Orc. And every day, a thousand Trainable endos, Climbers, came uptime to help prepare Earth against Doomsday.

Jerry Pierce advanced through the ranks quickly in those years, becoming something of a legend in the Agency. He would have been even more famous if the Agency hadn't been so reticent about his activities. After all, who but Pierce had directed the Turkish conquest of Constantinople, four centuries ahead of schedule? Who but Pierce had negotiated the oil-rights treaties between Petroleos Mexicanos and the Mayans? Who but Pierce had garroted an obscure Mongol chieftain named Temujin, before the man could become a problem?

And who but Pierce always carried a couple of chocolate bars, and dutifully wrote to his mother twice a month?

Three:

    The February evening fell in a flutter of wet snow that melted as it hit. New York glowed golden in the deepening grayness. For kilometer after kilometer, the highrises of Queens and Brooklyn blazed like pillars of fire. In some of the apartments, workers were just getting home, stripping off their clothes with sighs of relief, savoring the aroma of lamb chops or mastodon steak. After dinner, the Trainables could look forward to a pleasant evening of polychannel holovision; there was regular cinevision for the un-Trainables.

Most of the apartments were empty, though lights inside burned brightly. The custom was wasteful, of course, but it was good for morale. After the austerity years, lights had become as compulsive a luxury as the animal protein everyone ate in too-great quantities. Besides, lighting only the occupied flats would have made the city look like the ghost town it had become. Most New Yorkers had long since moved to the suburbs of the past, where even the humblest home squatted on a huge lot whose lawn took all weekend to mow. Not all the residents had gone willingly: two out of five were drafted emigrants who cursed the perfect weather of Tharman Egypt or Urthonan Brazil and yearned for the stink and uproar of Flatbush Tower's eighty-fifth floor.

The city streets were wet and quiet when computer programmer Eusebio Macapagal walked into a bar a few blocks from the Transferpoint Building, where he had just left work. Two men in rain ponchos followed him in. They watched him put away a big steam-table supper and a couple of liters of beer. They nodded to each other.

In the Transferpoint, there was a brief surge of traffic as the afternoon shift left and the evening shift came on. Most were Agency people, moving with easy confidence. At work, they sat in offices adorned with Doomsday plaques and holographs of Ulro, and composed memofiches to one another: we need seventy-five thousand Chinese farm workers on Vala by the end of next month; the Caliph of Baghdad has become a liability and must be removed; the World Anthropological Association has protested the Agency's treatment of endochronics on Los, and we must prepare a counterpropaganda campaign; we are calling a conference to discuss the rising Colonial birthrates. Each memo initiated an action, changed a million lives, founded or toppled an empire.

Austerity's children, they dressed soberly, even dully. The men tended to prefer checked tweed slacks, pleated white shirts, and blue or maroon blazers; the women, paisley-print sarongs or kilts and tunics. An occasional fop in embroidered denim strutted by, swinging his attaché case.

UnTrainable emigrants, en route downtime, of course wore Agency fatigues, but those returning to Earth on official business had taken pains to dress distinctively. A tall Black man glided across the Concourse in a gaudy yellow caftan, talking quietly with a Colonial Police officer. The Copo wore dress uniform: white tricorn with moa plumes, gold brocade jacket, and azure breeches tucked into knee boots. Such visitors affected a composure they rarely felt; anyone rude enough to make eye contact with a Colonial would probably find cold resentment glaring back at him.

Macapagal and the two men in ponchos entered the Concourse and strolled about for a time, windowshopping on the commercial mezzanine above the main floor. One of the men spoke quietly to Macapagal, who nodded absently.

Upstairs, on an Agency pistol range, Philon Richardson fired six flechettes into a five-centimeter bull's-eye. He studied the shot group for a moment, then ejected the empty clip from his Mallory .15, reloaded, and did it again. The pistol made an almost inaudible spitting sound.

On a still-higher floor, Wigner sipped sherry and studied the billiard table in his study. He loved the endless calculations, the estimates, the sheer precognition needed to put the balls where he wanted them, when he wanted them there, with the speed and spin he wanted. He was very good, but he played only against himself. His apartment was silent except for his good-tempered humming. He lived alone.

Pierce, wearing a beige corduroy Mao suit, took the elevator to Judy's apartment. His body was growing accustomed to the demands Dr. Suad had placed on it, and he found he could tune out most of the unwanted sensory input. Thank God.

Judy welcomed him with a hug. "Hi. I've missed you."

"Missed you too. Dinner smells good."

"It'll be awhile yet. Make yourself comfortable and I'll get you a beer." She turned on her heel and headed for the kitchen.

"Thanks." He removed his clothes and placed them in the wardrobe by the door. Trainables went about naked whenever possible. Returning to the room, he walked over to the holoprojector and riffled through the wall projections until he found a new one. The Mendocino cliffs on Ahania. He put it on two of the walls and the ceiling. The view was from the top of the black cliffs; waves smashed against the empty shore while gulls wheeled against the raw blue sky of early spring. Along the edge of the cliffs, grass and wildflowers bent in the wind from the sea. He muted the surf to a distant hiss.

"Put the salt on," Judy called from the kitchen, and

Pierce touched a button on the air conditioner. It was a close-to-perfect illusion, even to Pierce's heightened senses.

She returned carrying two steins of Löwenbräu, and they snuggled together on the couch to watch the waves break.

"You picked my new favorite. I hardly ever put on Pompeii or Macchu Picchu any more. But I can watch this for hours and hours."

"It's very pleasant. I still haven't spotted the recycle splice."

"It's a ten-minute cycle. Cost a fortune."

"Worth every cent," Pierce commented, then remembered something he had left in his pocket and went to the closet to retrieve it. "I brought you a present," he announced, and handed her a small square locket on a fine gold chain. "Bought it from a gold-smith in Philadelphia."

"It's beautiful! Thank you, love." She put it around her neck and turned to let him fasten the clasp. The gold sparkled against her tanned skin.

Pierce slouched farther down on the couch, enjoying the warmth of her body next to his, enjoying the wind in his hair and the sun on his face. "Well, love, how's life?"

"Very slow. Very quiet. No big actions, nobody coming home hurt. We're all dying of boredom."

"Eric's had me hyped to Grade Twelve, and blocked most of my Briefing."

She sat up, both surprised and concerned. "But you're going on a Colonial job."

"I am."

"Then—"

"Beats me. I suppose I'll learn why when I need to."

"But what's the sense of blocking an Agent for a Colonial mission?"

"Maybe there's more Secessionism in the air."

"On Orc?" She laughed. "Don't be silly—not with all those loyal scientists."

"Mm. Let's play chess."

"Sure."

They played quickly as old adversaries who could still outwit each other now and then. Pierce was surprised to beat her in twenty-five moves.

"I'll get my revenge after dinner," she threatened. "Between worrying about you and worrying about the meal, I can't concentrate."

"Nobody loves a whiny loser." Pierce grinned. "Let's eat."

As he expected, Judy had put together a good meal: hot-and-sour soup, tomato beef chow fun, green beans with pork and rice. Over coffee, Pierce described the cuisine he had been served at Monticello. "Corn bread, salt pork, and carrots. That was for guests. The old boy's got a freezer full of gourmet food, but they like to cling to their pioneer image in front of visitors."

After dinner they played some more chess, and Judy did indeed take her revenge by letting Pierce outsmart himself. He spent more time watching her than watching the board: she was tense and distracted.

"Now what's the matter," he finally asked after resigning the last game.

"Hm?"

"You know. You're all knotted up about something."

"It's you, Jerry. I'm afraid you'll come home hurt."

"We'll see. Not to worry." He put his arm around her shoulder and tried to comfort her.

"Comforted, but not completely satisfied, Judy led him toward the bedroom.

They made love, gently and slowly. Any intensity would prove to be too much for Pierce's overtuned body. His fingers and skin read her body, and the message was still there in her pulse and muscle—she was nervous and frightened, but excited as well, and not just by him.

Afterward, he relaxed in her arms, enjoying the smell of her hair. "I froze this morning," he confided to her.

She suddenly became very still, worried.

"I was getting off the shuttle from Beaulah. I froze. Just for a second."

"Are you sure?"

"I'm sure."

"Oh, Jerry. Did you tell Eric?"

"No. Not Suad, either. But Suad must know. You can't ever keep secrets from *him*. And if he knows, Eric knows."

Judy sat up, pulled away from Pierce, and turned to face him. "And they're sending you out anyway—"

"One last run. Waste not, want not. Then I can go rusticate and catch up on my reading."

"If you freeze again, at a bad time, you could get killed."

Pierce shrugged. "If I trip over my own feet, I could get killed, too."

"Are you scared," she asked.

"Sure." Pierce pushed the covers back and moved to the edge of the bed.

"What was it like?"

"Don't be morbid. Besides, it's time I left."

"Stay over, this once." She did not mean it.

"No thanks." He could not stand anyone else in bed with him while he slept. The very thought made him edgy.

Judy got out of bed and put on a simple black kimono. Pierce dressed, watching her watching him. She was just beginning to thicken, to lose her lean, hard dancer's waist and flat belly. He was sad to see her beginning to age. Then he realized she was studying him the same way. He laughed. "How'd we get so old, love? We're the whiz kids, aren't we?"

"Not any more, Jer. We're not kids playing games any more." She walked him to the door, her arm around his waist, her head against his shoulder. He confirmed what he had suspected: she was upset, frightened, yet detached. He was in danger; she knew it, but wasn't warning him except through the smell and texture of her skin, the pattern of her eye movements, the subtle tensions of a body under too much control.

"See you soon." He smiled, kissing her lightly as she opened the door.

"Bye, Jerry."

The door closed, and he stood alone in the quiet corridor. Then he walked slowly toward the elevators, past several intersecting corridors. Nearing the last intersection, he smelled orange blossoms, and had a whiff of beer. On one side of the intersection, he realized, someone was waiting to kill him. Which side? Left—the orange-blossom scent was stronger there. How many? Only one? Yes.

Pierce stepped into the intersection, catching a glimpse of the man out of the corner of his eye. A pistol glinted and sighed; a flechette kissed the air over Pierce's head as he dropped, spun to face the man from a sprinter's crouch, and leaped.

The man was short and thickset, with an impassive expression on his round brown face. In a fair fight he might have been a dangerous opponent, but this was not a fair fight. The man stank of orange blossoms—he had been doped with hypnine to slow his reflexes. Before the man could correct his aim, Pierce broke his wrist. The pistol fell to the carpeted floor, Pierce kicked it down the hall and extended the kick into the man's groin.

The man groaned, tried to say something, then collapsed. Pierce gripped him by the shirtfront and swung him head first into the wall. About three seconds had elapsed since the flechette was fired.

Pierce went through his attacker's pockets, found nothing. The pistol was equally anonymous, a cheap plastic job with a rough finish intended to mask fingerprints. Pierce sighed and turned on his ringmike.

"Eric? Jerry. Sorry to bother you at home, but some fellow's just tried to kill me."

"Where are you?"

"The hundred and twenty-second floor, Southwest, Corridor J. There's no ID on him, and he's full of hypnine."

"Cat's-paw. Okay, call Security to come sweep him up. Are you all right?"

"Thought you'd never ask. Yeah. Adrenalin high on Grade Twelve reflexes is rough, though."

"Of course."

The unconscious man had been mugged, doped, and parked in the corridor with orders to fire at someone resembling Pierce. The real killer was far away; his cat's-paw would not even remember being accosted, let alone how his wrist came to be broken. Pierce felt sorry for the man, doubtless an innocent citizen whose life had been so casually appropriated without his consent.

"Who would want me dead?" Pierce murmured into the mike.

"Don't know, Jerry."

Pierce wished he could see Wigner. Over the earphone his boss's voice sounded untrustworthy, but it was hard to be certain.

"What am I getting into tomorrow?"

"You seem to be in it already. Don't worry, Jerry. Your subconscious will let you know what you need to know when you need to know it. Damned safer this way."

"I know. I know."

Pierce meant it. He trusted Wigner; he always had.

Four:

One never called them Backsliders. Emigrants, pioneers, settlers, redeployed developmental and support personnel—but never Backsliders. They called themselves that, but Homebodies and Climbers had to maintain a genteel courtesy toward the people they deported.

Pierce often wondered why these people resented being moved. Downtime, the air was clean, the water sweet. Fortunes were being made in hundreds of industries. Yet they resented it. In '09, seventy thousand Calcuttans died in the Ten-Week Riot against the transfer of half the city's population to Ahania. The received wisdom in the Agency was that the emigrants' morale rose as their new homes began to resemble their old ones in squalor and misery. Much philosophizing was heard in Agency offices about the perversity of human nature.

At 0545, scarcely six hours since the cat's-paw —identified as Eusebio Macapagal, a Trainable-Gamma employee of the Agency—had attacked him, Pierce felt rested and alert. His B&C helped induce optimum sleep sequences, reducing his normal seven hours' requirement to four. Pierce woke, dressed, packed, and dropped to the Concourse in twenty minutes. At this hour, the plaza was nearly empty.

His documents got him through Intertemporal Customs at once past a long line of sleepy emigrants. He rode the escalator down into a tunnel just like the one to Beulah. The platform was already crowded with emigrants. They huddled on the benches that ran the length of the tunnel, or sprawled on the cement floor amid their luggage.

They smelled. They jabbered, coughed, spat, smoked, pissed in the trash cans, laughed, wept, whined, snarled. They wore fatigues; Pierce wore a brown duffel coat over a brown-and-white sweater and tan slacks. They fell silent as he picked his way through the crowd, then joked about him once he had passed.

Pierce did not mind—this oral abuse was only the equivalent of the graffiti they were allowed to spray on the shuttle cars. He found an empty space between an old woman snoring on the platform, using a suitcase for a pillow, and a young couple. The young man clutched a blue vinyl folder that held their emigration orders, IDs, immunization records, credit cards, and travel tickets. He was probably nineteen; the girl, obviously his new wife, seemed to be a year or so younger.

With a grunt and a yawn, Pierce hunkered down. He turned to the young couple and smiled. He had a lovely smile, bright, humorous, and infectious, and he knew it. The couple, expecting to ignore him and to be ignored in turn, were surprised and subtly flattered.

"Hi. My name's Jerry. Where are you two bound for?"

Shaking his hand, the man responded cordially. "I'm Pete, and this is Jenny. My wife. We're s'posed to be going to Nueva Merida. Uh, what about you?"

"Business trip to the west coast. Nueva Merida, huh? I hear it's a great town." Pierce looked over at Pete's wife. "You two going to settle there?"

"Well—Jenny's brother lives there," Pete answered. "He offered me a job on his fishing boat. Guess it beats just being sent any old place."

"Sounds good. Things are booming all around the Gulf. Fishing, oil, farming—you name it. You'll make out fine."

"I sure better." Pete sighed. "Then we can go buy a little island somewheres, and me and Jenny can live there and not have to worry about AID or Doomsday or nothin'."

Jenny looked scared; Pierce was obviously no emigrant and therefore was a Trainable. But Pete was emboldened by his nearness to Orc, as well as by Pierce's friendliness.

"Sorry to leave Earth, huh?" Pierce asked.

"Hell. I had a good job with the New Haven City Schools—custodian's aide. And Jenny was doin' real good in vocational school, doin' Homecraft. But just 'cause we got married, bam, okay, kids, here's your walking papers." He waved the vinyl folder. "They wouldn't even let Jenny finish school. You know, we was too honest. Shoulda got married secretly."

"*Honey,* you *know* it wouldn' of worked," Jenny objected. "*Any*body our age gets married, they know about it."

"Well, live together, then."

Jenny gasped; the boy blushed at his own gaucherie. Pierce was amused by the growing priggishness of the younger generation.

"They'd prob'ly learn 'bout that too," Jenny mumbled. "My folks sure would, anyways," she added with a nervous giggle.

"Just not fair. Know what my IQ is?" Pete asked. "One twenty-two. My counselor tol' me when I turned sixteen and I was goin' in for Testing. Heck, I was smarter than lots of kids, but that flickertube—wow, I could never make any sense of that in a million years."

"Well, only about twelve percent are Trainables," Pierce observed. "It's just one of those things you're born with, like your blood type."

"Sit under the dumb thing for fifteen minutes and that's all, kid, thank you, and kiss your future goodbye."

"Petey, honey, *please.*" Jenny was embarrassed, but her husband listened to her no more than he did to Pierce.

"Just not fair."

"You're kidding me." Pierce grinned. "Your wife was studying to be a domestic servant in some rich family's house, and you were holding a janitor's broom for him. On Orc you'll own your own house in less than a year. And you'll be making more money in a month than you'd make in a year if you stayed here."

Pete turned a level gaze on him.

"Sure. And I can sit in front of the cinevision every night and watch blinkies like you tell each other what to do about duds like us."

Blinkies—a new term of insult. They coined a few more every week. Pierce shrugged, smiled faintly, and turned away. So much for the screened loyals who were the only ones allowed to settle on Orc.

"Attention, please. Attention, please." A pleasant female voice came over the PA system and made everyone sit up and start fussing with their belongings. "Emigrants to Orc, please board cars two, three, four, and five. Nonemigrant passengers, please board car one only. Line up at the orange turnstiles and board the shuttle promptly when they open. Thank you—and have a *good time*."

Some of the emigrants cheered, sarcastically; most lined up silently. Pierce discovered he was the only nonemigrant, a situation that was not unusual.

Shuttles were necessary because I-Screens demanded a great deal of power and broke down within a few minutes unless carefully maintained. For a shuttle trip, the Screen was on for only fifteen seconds, and as many people as possible had to be hurled through in that time. After thousands of trips, Pierce was as intrigued as ever by the process and remained standing at the front of the empty car, looking out the window toward the end of the tunnel.

Ten meters down the track, they came to a wall, its tiled mosaic interrupted by a circular metal band half a meter wide and glinting a dull gold. The circle, six meters in diameter, curved just under the tracks. As Pierce watched, the golden circle brightened. A chime sounded somewhere outside, and the mosaic within the circle disappeared. In its place, a soap-bubble film swirled for an instant before it, too, vanished, revealing a tunnel that was the mirror image of this one. A puff of wind gusted against the window as air pressures equalized.

The shuttle banged forward through the circle; the only sensation was the thin click of the car going over the suddenly joined rails where the two tunnels merged. The shuttle stopped, having traveled about sixty meters, and the doors opened. Six burly Immigration officers in blue-and-white uniforms paced the platform. They wore sidearms, Pierce observed with surprise.

"Arright, arright, people," the leader bellowed, "give us five lines facing this way. Come on, hustle! We ain't got all night."

Thirty seconds before, they had been emigrants; now they were immigrants. As they milled about on the platform, many looked back down the tunnel. The I-Screen was gone. There was no mosaic on this side; blank concrete and fourteen thousand years divided them from Earth. Pierce saw Pete and Jenny, caught their eye, and waved good-bye. Pete looked down. Jenny waved back, smiling uncertainly.

The Immigration sergeant glanced at Pierce's documents and saluted. "Need a hand with that bag, sir?"

"No thanks."

"Fujimura—get upstairs and hold a cab for this gentleman."

The slim Japanese nodded and sprinted upstairs; Pierce was graciously grateful to the sergeant.

The Concourse here was much less impressive than the one uptime. The plaza was a forest of pillars, with bare concrete underfoot and overhead. The shops and restaurants made little effort to attract customers, having an assured clientele. Most of the shuttle entrances were sealed, since this was a minor Transferpoint on Orc, and saw mostly immigrant traffic from Earth. Over the main entrance, a garish sign fluoresced in blue on white:

WELCOME TO ORC—
ARSENAL OF HUMANKIND!
Local Time: 0347 EST 8 Feb 2015 AD
Absolute Time: 0347 EST 7 Apr 12, 165 BC
Rent-a-Car from Hertz-Avis

Pierce paused at an all-night fichemonger's to pick up some novels and a dozen local papers and magazines. Slipping them into his duffel coat, he went outside into a raw, blustery night. Fujimura stood shivering beside a cab, an ancient Chevy Scooter.

"Thanks for your trouble." Pierce smiled, handing the Immigration man a ten-dollar tip. "You fellas have breakfast on me."

The sleepy cabby drove him to the jetport, about where La Guardia Field once was on Earth. The roads were slippery; there was a freezing wind roaring south from the dying glaciers of New England. They drove through kilometers of drab houses—"Two-Family Ranchettes," the brochures called them—with big, unkempt yards and double-glazed windows. This neighborhood could be part of any Western Colony on any chronoplane, Pierce reflected.

He had a three-hour wait at the jetport. After breakfast, finding little to interest him in the jetport terminal, he rented a privacy booth for an hour and read: Dickens, Lessing, Stacton. Really, all this waiting was a waste of time. But it gave him time to think about what he had seen so far.

The changes he had noticed this morning were not pleasant. The young immigrant's surliness: sloppy screening had allowed him onto a very sensitive chronoplane. The Immigration officers: rude and overbearing to everyone but himself, and wearing sidearms. The few people about, both at the Transferpoint and in the terminal, seemed angry and apathetic. Many cast cold looks at him after he left his booth and waited in the departure lounge. Pierce was used to being disliked, but the obviousness and intensity of that dislike were new and striking. Had they all forgotten why they were here? And, thinking that, he realized he had seen virtually no Doomsday posters.

The jet finally departed a little after dawn. It was an old Ilyushin, less than half full though it would be the only transcontinental flight of the day. Every Agency airline was a money-loser, of course. Orc, for example, had a Colonial population of seventy-two million, plus five or ten million endos. Scattered in urban clusters and small towns, the Colonies would stagnate without some fast transport.

Across Pennsylvania and Ohio there was little to see but a thin subglacial forest, mostly scrub pine. Countless lakes, most of them small, interrupted the woods, and there was still plenty of snow. For a time Pierce could glimpse Lake Warren—what would eventually be the Great Lakes was now a single immense inland sea, its icy surface blazing in the spring sun.

The forest thickened near the Mississippi, with a raw, logged-off stretch around a lumber town here and there. There were a few roads—local transport was usually by helicopter or river-going hovercraft.

The plane made half a dozen stops between Glaciopolis and Little St. Louis, the largest city in the Midwest. The settlement hadn't changed much since Pierce's last visit—it remained a sprawl of tractvilles around the domed core. But there was an unmistakable brown haze mantling it. Smog. He made a mental note to report the matter when he got back. Colonials! Give them a pristine new world and they wrecked it in half a generation.

The prairies looked almost exactly like those of Earth, an infinite plain geometrized into megafarms. Under the spring snow, the first of the year's three wheat crops was beginning to sprout. Though the land looked thickly settled, there were in fact fewer farmers than loggers on Orc. Those immense wheatfields were tended by a few lonely men and women and their automated equipment.

Pierce looked out the window for a while, dozed, then turned to the newsfiches he had picked up in Glaciopolis. The *New Orc Times* was typically Colonial, from its punny title to its trivial content. Most of the paper was reprinted from uptime media; by the time Pierce waded through all two hundred pages, he had absorbed most of yesterday's Earth news but learned little of local events. Dropping the 'fiche in the recycle bin under his seat, he turned to another paper. It was the same, a mass of trivia—horoscopes, gossip, recipes, comics, warmed-over news items from Earth.

The sheer consistency of the two papers interested him, however. He read the rest of his newsfiches with a scholar's detached attentiveness. In three minutes he was through.

There was virtually no hard news about Orc. Commissioner Gersen's name was mentioned often, but only in stories obviously ground out in some press secretary's office. He could find no local criticism of the Colonial administration, a remarkable state of affairs on any downtime world, where public bitching was a popular pastime. Pierce felt the scholar's detached pleasure in a hypothesis confirmed—a media fog was operating. It was less obvious than outright censorship, but just as effective, as the Agency had reason to know. Pierce wondered why this one had been created, and by whom. If his Briefing had not been blocked, he suspected, there would be no need to wonder.

The glaciated Rockies lay smothered under storms. West of the Deseret Sea, he could see little sign of settlement, though brushfires indicated the locations of endo tribes, which set them to drive game into convenient hunting grounds. Just like Colonials, Pierce thought, always quick to seize a short-term gain even at the cost of a long-term disaster.

Once past the Sierra Nevada, the plane flew over inhabited country again. The foothills sloped down to the countless farms and ranches of the Nuevo Sacramento

Valley. The Ilyushin began dropping quickly, and as they descended over the Alcatraz Valley Pierce was surprised to see it dotted with truck farms and summer cottages, none of which had been there during the Secessionist business in '12.

He glimpsed Little Frisco, a hamlet existing only for its Transferpoint to Earth, and then they started their descent into the airport in the dunes east of Farallon City. In a thousand years or so, melting glaciers would flood this beautiful, bleak coastal plain and roll through the Golden Gate Pass into the Alcatraz Valley. Until that time, the Farallon Coast would be one of the loveliest places on all the chronoplanes.

Waiting in the brown-and-gold arrival lounge was a solidly built, impassive man with tranquil blue eyes and shiny pink skin. Pierce walked directly up to him and extended his hand. "Harry McGowan, I presume."

Commissioner Gersen's Director of Security Services smiled faintly, then nodded. "Very pleased to meet you, sir." McGowan had a Rhodesian accent, which had to be an affectation; the whites had been out of Zimbabwe for a generation, and McGowan himself had been on Orc for over ten years. "Hope you had a good flight."

"Mm, fine."

"If it's no inconvenience, the Commissioner would like to speak with you before you go on to Los Alamitos."

"Of course."

They walked out into the main mall of the terminal, busy with travelers and officials. Pierce was grimly pleased to see the number of plainclothes Colonial Police stationed strategically around the mall. He did not know what was going on, but it was clear that something unpleasant was taking place here on Orc.

Located just off the mall was a small office suite used by the airport administrators, who had been evicted today to make room for Gersen and a high-ranking Copo in uniform. Bengt Gersen was a large, powerful-looking man of forty-five whose Habsburg chin gave him a somewhat bovine expression. As he rose from his chair to shake Pierce's hand, Gersen's paunch jutted out oddly under his maroon blazer. Pierce, recognizing the bulge as one that would be made by a personal computer, looked for the thin scar behind Gersen's ear where the speakout terminal would be implanted. Finding it, he felt a grudging respect for Gersen: not every unTrainable was bright enough or quick enough to handle a personal computer's whispering advice.

The Copo was Colonel Li Shih, a very handsome Canadian-born Chinese of medium height. He wore his gaudy uniform with grace, and smiled as he was introduced to Pierce.

"Mr. Pierce," said Gersen, "let me say at the outset how pleased and honored we are by your agreeing to investigate this situation."

"You're very kind, Commissioner. I hope I shall be of some use."

"We have every confidence in your branch of the Agency. I'm sure you'll have the saboteurs apprehended very quickly."

"If there are any." Pierce smiled.

Gersen looked surprised. "You did read my report to your superior?"

"Thoroughly."

"We feel the evidence is overwhelming," Colonel Shih said.

"More than overwhelming," snapped McGowan. "Bloody irrefutable."

Pierce raised an eyebrow at him. McGowan leaned forward in his chair.

"Think about it, Mr. Pierce. Their methods are very subtle, but the pattern's there when you look. The boffins keep reporting bugs in their instrumentation, odd delays in tests, unexpected results that send them back to their blackboards, or—whatever they use. Little things, but they all add up to the impression that the project isn't worth following up on, that the basic theory's wrong, that the project's too expensive—that sort of thing. Christ, they even worry about ecological effects. As a result, we dropped several projects before we smelled smoke."

"Forgive me, but all this sounds terribly subjective to me," Pierce replied.

"Then let me give you some very objective facts, Mr. Pierce," McGowan retorted. "*Item*: the 3,4-hyperpyrase program. A solid fuel for the Gnat micromissile. They couldn't develop the fuel to more than thirty percent of theoretical efficiency. Scrapped the whole program last summer.

"*Item*: the ZOMBI long-range detection system. Six years' work on that one, Mr. Pierce. By now it ought to be able to spot a tennis ball a light-year away, and tell you what color it is. In practice we're lucky if it can find Jupiter on a clear night.

"*Item*: high-temperature superconductors. We know they had them uptime, but after four years' effort we can't begin to duplicate them." He paused. "Shall I go on?"

"Thank you, but you've made your point. These projects—and the others mentioned in the commissioner's report—are all pretty remote from one another, aren't they? Have there been any WDS people working on all these projects?"

"In some cases, but not all," McGowan said. "When a project is shelved, its people usually move to another one. On the long-term projects, the senior people almost never transfer, but the juniors certainly do. And of course everyone socializes and talks shop. I believe that's called the interdisciplinary approach," McGowan added contemptuously.

"So this supposed sabotage could be caused by a handful of scientists moving from project to project."

"Theoretically," Shih responded. "Mr. McGowan asked us to correlate personnel shifts with aborted projects, but we came up with nothing very solid."

Gersen cleared his throat. "As I'm sure you're

aware, Mr. Pierce, the Weapons Development Site is off limits to unauthorized individuals, but movement within the Site is quite easy, despite its size. That's the policy the scientists demanded, and I'm not criticizing it, not for a moment. But it does mean that a small group—even a single individual—could gain access to all the projects thus far affected."

Pierce said nothing for a moment. "Have you any suspects, Mr. McGowan?"

"Plenty. Too many."

"What is that supposed to mean?" Pierce asked, rapidly becoming interested.

"We've a very mixed bag down there. Lots of Climbers, lots of odds and sods from Earth. Mob of Mexican Indians from Beulah, some Romans from Ahania, a few Arabs, a mad Greek or two. And of course we've got Anita !Kosi. All of 'em are Trained, of course, so there *shouldn't* be any questions about their loyalty . . ."

"You think otherwise?"

McGowan looked uncomfortable. "Let's say I beg to differ with the usual faith in Training. Everyone likes to think that it's all or nothing, you've got Trainability or you don't. Well, maybe so when it comes to pumping in raw data. But what about emotional attitudes, cultural values? You can take some savage out of the jungle and teach him physics, but can you really teach him loyalty? Teamwork? Excuse me, but I bloody well doubt it."

Gersen looked embarrassed. "With all due respect, Mr. McGowan, I think you may be overstating the case. We can all agree that there is a likelihood that, among twenty-five thousand Trained scientists, there are some disaffected persons who may be engaging in sabotage. Now—"

"I don't agree." Pierce allowed the hint of a sneer to creep into his voice. Gersen paused. They all looked at him.

"First of all, Mr. McGowan's views on Training are

comparable to a blind man's opinion of Picasso. Secondly, it is just as easy to Train people's emotions as it is to Train their intellects. But it is also highly illegal, as you all should know. Agency regulations state that any Trainee who demonstrates disloyalty, or refuses to freely accept Earth values, is automatically Cleared of Training and returned to his home culture. There have been several cases where this procedure was invoked. So Mr. McGowan is groundlessly impugning the loyalty of WDS personnel.

"And if there are no grounds for suspecting those persons," Pierce went on, "the sabotage theory falls apart. The alternative theories may be less dramatic, but are more likely."

"Such as?" asked Shih quietly.

"Sloppy administration. Poor project supervision. Too much money. The WDS gets all the funding it asks for—sometimes even more—and anyone with a plausible idea can usually get backing. We support a lot of schemes that turn out to be harebrained, in the hope that some of them just might work out after all."

"Do you favor any of these . . . alternative theories?"

"No, Colonel; I try to keep an open mind. If I find evidence of real sabotage, I will of course take appropriate measures. But I do not expect to find such evidence."

He looked at his watch.

"My plane leaves in five minutes. Thank you for arranging this meeting, gentlemen. I'll be in touch."

He stood up, shook hands with each of them, then left the office. As he walked out, he found himself sweating. Each of the men in the room wanted to kill him; at least, their bodies and faces conveyed that message. He would discount that—such paranoid thoughts having been inspired by several people in the last twenty-four hours—except that he had, after all, been attacked by a cat's-paw last night.

What was more, *he* had wanted to kill *them*. It had

taken a conscious effort to keep from pulling his pistol and murdering them all. Pierce was not upset by that impulse, but he wondered very much why he had been Briefed to have it.

Five:

Los Alamitos stood about where Santa Monica did fourteen thousand years uptime, but it was well inland and sheltered from the sea by a five-kilometer strip of dunes, chaparral, and scrub pine. With its adobe houses and quiet streets, it reminded Pierce of Taos in the '80s. It did not look like a research center, despite the tedious functionalism of some of the larger buildings. After his long trip, Pierce felt very much at home here, where virtually everyone was Trainable.

Eugene Younger, Director of the WDS, met him on the tarmac of Oppenheimer Field. Younger wore baggy khaki trousers, a red flannel shirt, and a leather jacket—a red baseball cap was shoved into his hip pocket. He was tall, slim and tanned, with a graying brown beard and a receding hairline, though he was only twenty-five.

"So you're Pierce," he said as Pierce stepped off the plane. "I'm Gene. Where to?"

"Everywhere."

"Good. The chopper's on the other side."

As they walked around the terminal building, Pierce decided he liked Younger. Many Trainables, including Pierce, were insulated by their status and developed an impenetrable reserve; it was a way of coping with being very young and very powerful. Younger, though, seemed unashamedly boyish, unclouded by cynicism. Whereas Pierce walked in a controlled glide, Younger bounced.

The helicopter was a two-man Merwin Pipit that

lifted almost noiselessly into the air. Younger flew it with elegance.

"Lots of changes in five years," he remarked as they climbed.

"It's grown," Pierce agreed. He had been here at the WDS only once before, in '10, when a previous Director had been coping with hostile endos. "Still smoggy."

"Damned inversion layer. The L.A. Basin's impossible on every chronoplane."

They swept north to the mountains, then east. Most of the WDS was centered in Los Alamitos, but test ranges and special facilities were scattered clear across southern California to the Colorado. The terrain was green and brown, broad grasslands interrupted by dense stands of oak and pine. Rivers and creeks glinted in the sun, and there were many lakes and marshes—all fed by the storm track that would eventually move north as the glaciers receded. Pierce recognized the installations they passed over: Nuclear Weapons Fabrication, Laser Research, the immense elliptical antennas of the ZOMBI station. After a long empty stretch, they approached the Mojave Verde Missile Facility, the center for spaceflight research and development.

The Facility, larger than it had been five years before, was a sprawling grid of streets and buildings separated from the launching pads and missile-assembly center by a low ridge. Some kilometers away, Pierce saw smoke on the hills.

"So the endos are back."

"No trouble now. No real trouble, that is."

"Ah?"

"They steal a lot. Even inside the Facility. Don't ask me how they get through the wire and the detection system. But at least they don't kill." He grinned at Pierce, mischievously. "We caught one a few weeks ago. Told him we'd call back the Deathwalker if they didn't quit raiding us, and sent him back to Klasayat."

"Klasayat!" Pierce was both pleased and mortified. Five years ago, the Grasslanders had been a serious nuisance, and their leader, Klasayat, had shown great skill in conducting a guerilla war with stolen weapons. Likable, troublesome people. Pierce had regretted having to direct their extermination. Oddly enough, they had liked him too. They had called him Jerry Missanan'kaa, the Deathwalker—high praise. But how had any of them escaped the spectrum of plagues he had spread across their territory? Professionally, Pierce was embarrassed; personally, he was glad. He rarely had the chance to respect his opponents.

"I guess I'll have to finish them off once and for all."

"Don't bother. They keep us on our toes. And Klasayat's days are numbered. Their last women died almost a year ago; his boys will be drifting off pretty soon."

Cold consolation; Pierce hated a sloppy kill.

A small jet fighter appeared out of nowhere and circled the Pipit like a hawk intercepting a dragonfly. Younger murmured a code phrase into his throat mike; the jet turned away and vanished into the sun.

"Very touchy about intruders," Pierce observed.

"Too touchy. We inherited most of the old military paranoia. Not much to be paranoid about—most of the space projects are pure research. Unmanned probes to the outer planets, radio astronomy, that kind of thing." He looked mildly embarrassed. "Anita !Kosi was working here for a while, but Seamus Brown asked to have her transferred." Brown was the supervisor of the Facility, and a very, very good rocket engineer.

Pierce looked puzzled.

"Internal politics. She began demanding too much for her pet project—research into hypermagnetic fields for radio astronomy."

"Project Sherlock." Pierce recognized the name from his Briefing. It made him tense, though he didn't know why. But in Younger he could discern no tension, only the annoyance of an administrator compelled to expedient measures despite himself.

"Right. It was costing a fortune. Seamus Brown's still supporting the project, but he cut the hell out of the budget." He looked at Pierce and shrugged. "I could please Anita and disrupt everyone else, or move her. Temporarily. So that's what I did. There's no lack of work here for a genius."

The Pipit curved away from the skeletal gantries of Mojave Verde, back toward the coast. Pierce could see other installations: the Institute for Ulronic Studies, where scavenged items were examined and puzzled over; the Biotronics Lab, where cyborgs were built and dismantled; the Materials Research Unit; and the Intense Fields Station, where even gravity sometimes faded or tilted.

"I see one big change since '05," said Pierce.

"Yes?"

"You're doing basic research all over the WDS, not just building weapons."

"That's no secret—but we don't publicize the fact."

"Why?"

"Suppose the British were warned in 1910 that the Germans would one day attack them with long-range bombers and guided missiles. What sort of defenses could the Brits have come up with? Dirigibles against V-2s? Their best bet would be to push pure science, and screw the secret weapons for a few years until they'd learned something. Without anyone saying so out loud, that's what we've decided. Oh, the weapons stuff goes on, but no one's very interested."

"Pacifists?"

Younger laughed delightedly. "No, no, they want really *nasty* weapons, not just death rays. They'd like to build movable black holes you could drop a planet into, but we don't know enough to do *that* yet. So all the brightest people are in basic research."

"You're *all* saboteurs!"

"In a way. But Gersen's famous memo is a pile of shit. He's a bright man, for an unTrainable, but he and his people see conspiracies when it's just home-style entropy at work. The bastard has got us twitching, though."

"The memo's increased his influence here?"

"Yes, unfortunately. And it was already considerable."

"Why?"

"Gersen's a parallel power to me. Most of our funding comes directly from the International Federation, administered by AID. But the Colonies invest in us, too, and Gersen's their broker."

"Of course." Pierce recalled several WDS projects initiated by Colonial governments: Thel wanted to create ice-free harbors north of 45°; Los wanted better seismic predictions and improved storage batteries.

"So Gersen influences events here."

"Very much so. Even some of my senior people owe him favors; when he wants something, they help him get it."

"Such as?"

"Usually it's lubrication for some colonial project—more people, improved computer access, that sort of stuff. Gersen retains a lot of clout among the Colonial bureaucrats, because he can make Trainables do his bidding."

"His politics?"

"Impeccably bland."

"I doubt it," Pierce said as the Pipit whirred softly down to the roof of the Holiday Inn in downtown Los Alamitos. Younger looked sharply at him.

"The son of a bitch is up to something," said Pierce. "I don't know what, but it's probably treasonous."

"Strong talk."

Pierce did not reply. He pulled his suitcase out from behind the seat and clambered down onto the helicopter pad. Then he leaned back into the Pipit. "I want the full records of every Colonial research project, past and present. Dossiers on everyone connected with those projects, including the Colonial liaison people. Oh, and dossiers on every Copo on Orc, past and present. Okay?"

Younger nodded. "When?"

"By 1900 hours."

"No pain."

"One more thing. I want four absolutely reliable people from your own Security team—not from McGowan. One here on the roof, one roving the hotel, two outside my room. Get 'em in place as soon as possible."

"It's that serious?"

"Yes."

"They'll be on their way in five minutes."

"Good. I may want to see you again sometime tonight, but for sure we should meet tomorrow morning."

"When?"

"When we decide which projects to suspend and whom to put under arrest."

Younger grinned and waved good-bye. The Pipit lifted off as Pierce headed downstairs to his room. He began visualizing its layout and approaches, the points in neighboring buildings which overlooked it. The room was not as protected as he would have liked, but it would do. It had to. To change rooms would involve trusting unTrainable hotel employees, and Pierce now trusted no such person on Orc.

Younger was as good as his word. The four guards—one woman, three men—arrived almost as soon as Pierce did. They were calm, relaxed, nondescript, and they listened well. Pierce assigned them to their stations and took a catnap until the first of several messengers arrived with cartons of microfiches. Though facsimile transmissions direct to his room could have been arranged, they might have been monitored.

The afternoon wore into evening as Pierce flickread through thousands of documents, pausing only for a perfunctory supper. He read them in no particular order, knowing his subconscious would file and organize everything. By 2200 hours, he knew a very great deal about every WDS project ever funded by Colonial governments; he was familiar with the records of every scientist and technician associated with those projects and he had reviewed the records of every Colonial

Police officer on Orc since the Copos had been established here.

Several items interested him. First, the involvement of Anita !Kosi in Project Sherlock. She was, of course, one of the most renowned scientists on any chronoplane. Together with the fifteen other members of her family, she was justification enough for the entire Testing and Recruitment Program, for the !Kosis were *all* Trainables, even those who were already adults when Tested. They were Boskopoids, big-brained ancestors of the Bushman peoples from Luvah, and in the decade since their discovery they had made a dozen major contributions to science. If Anita !Kosi was interested in Sherlock, there had to be value in the project. If she had been removed, the pressure on Younger must have been intense. Intense enough to make him prefer the scandal that would erupt if the removal were publicized.

Pierce had no doubt about the chief source of that pressure: Seamus Brown. Judging by his thick file, Brown was a complex man: four marriages and any number of sexual liaisons; membership both in scientific societies and in some crank groups. Though he privately dismissed the alien-invader Doomsday theory, he publicly exploited it to sustain IF funding of his missile programs. Did not drink or smoke. Played squash once a week with Harry McGowan, among others, but made insulting remarks about McGowan to Trainables. Ran the Missile Facility with a heavy hand, and generally got results.

Project Sherlock itself was clever, but seemed nothing special. Using a hint or two found in some Ulronian documents, a team led by Anita !Kosi had developed a modified hypermagnetic generator and had four of them installed in a Daedalus missile. After launch, the missile was to be placed in stationary orbit whereupon the generators would be turned on and dispersed. In theory that would create a very large field—a kind of magnetic lens millions of kilometers in diameter, capable of focusing electromagnetic radiation from the most distant galaxies—and of picking up any artificial radio signals originating within a thousand light-years. That capability, presumably, had ensured approval for the project; radio astronomy had flourished for years thanks to public fear of alien invaders. But Pierce saw nothing notable in Sherlock, apart from some technical details and the fact that it was prodigiously expensive. Politics again. Someone—probably Seamus Brown, possibly others as well—was using the project for private purposes. Pierce did not waste time spinning theories about Sherlock; the facts would come to light in due course.

The Copo files yielded much more interesting information. Three years ago, Pierce had exposed a Secessionist network in the Colonial Police here. Most of its members had been older men, former officers in the armies of Earth who had preferred rustication downtime to alcoholic retirement in Arizona, the Balearics, or the Crimea. UnTrainables, of course, and still soaked in their smelly little nationalisms, they had concocted a few imaginary grievances and begun to plan a coup. Once they were in control of Orc, they had deceived themselves, the International Federation would treat them as a sovereign state and agree to relax Agency policies in exchange for continued immigration and trade. That was a persistent fantasy among Colonials, one that had provided plenty of work for Agents like Pierce.

The plot had been as thickheaded as its authors, and Pierce had had no trouble rounding up all two hundred conspirators before they could take any action. A few had been sent to penal colonies, but most had been cashiered and kicked off Orc to less sensitive worlds. The Copos as a force were in disgrace and had been replaced in the WDS by Site Security, a Trainable corps.

Six months later, however, Gersen had established a Copo Special Reserve, and within a year almost a hundred of the former Secessionists had enlisted. They had drifted back to Orc by one means or another: with official pardons, under assumed identities, perhaps even through the illegal I-Screens used by knotholers. The Special Reserves had been moved quietly about since then, and in the past six months most had been based in Farallon City, engaging in little more than small-arms training. To Pierce, they looked like the nucleus of a putsch. A suicidal putsch, since AID's armed forces could crush the combined Colonies in a day, pouring men and machines onto every chronoplane from a hundred I-Screens.

He put down his flickreader, got up from his arm-chair, and walked in slow, controlled steps up and down the room, automatically avoiding the windows. He wanted very much to smash something. It was not the putsch that infuriated him; it was the gross incompetence that had allowed it to get this far. In the old days, when he had been a T-Colonel, he had known everything, *everything*, that went on in his district. It had been said with little exaggeration that if two hookers exchanged political opinions at midnight in the ladies' room of the sleaziest bar in Mountain Home, Pierce would know it by morning.

But now Trainable slovenliness had encouraged this threat to one of the most important installations on twelve chronoplanes. Trainables had allowed disgruntled settlers to colonize; they had ignored Gersen's formation of a private Copo army of convicted traitors; they had ignored a media fog clumsy enough to be spotted by any Trainable at a glance; and they had allowed unTrainables to exert influence on WDS scientists, even on a !Kosi. Incredible!

The scandal would be massive. Pierce took some consolation in that. There would be questions asked in the IF Assembly. AID was overdue for a purge and a tightening up, and this mess would provide ample justification. Wigner might even let some of the details leak to the media.

—*Wigner knows already.*

The thought slipped away, almost like a dream forgotten in waking, and Pierce had to fight to get it back.

Wigner knows already, or knows a lot. That's why I'm blocked, because Gersen's boys might pick me up. And that's why I wanted to kill Gersen and Shih and McGowan—because once I've got the goods on them, they'll need killing.

Pierce had a headache. After speaking briefly with one of the guards in the hall, he went to bed. Why, then, did Gersen *ask* the Agency to intervene? What's with all this sabotage crap?

He slept poorly, and rose early. In the early dawn, Los Alamitos was still and lovely, its broad streets empty except for an occasional Copo patrol car. The Santa Monica Mountains, crested with snow, glowed pink in the first rays of the sun. It was a beautiful world. They all were.

Pierce dressed and went out to dismiss his guards. Then he walked downstairs to the parking basement, where Younger had left a Toyota sedan for his use. A quick check showed no one had tampered with it. He drove out, headed for Younger's home.

The Director lived in Palisades, a beach suburb of Los Alamitos. His rambling cedar house stood on a low cliff above the cold blue sea; along the foot of the cliff, a narrow sandy beach stretched for kilometers without a footprint. The nearest neighbor was half a kilometer away.

Pierce interrupted breakfast; Younger brought him into a glass-walled kitchen whose table was set for two. There was a hint of perfume in the air.

"Chloe doesn't like dealing with people this early in the day," Younger said. "In any case, I presume she wouldn't be interested in what you have to say." He smiled, pouring Pierce some coffee.

"And what *do* I have to say?"

"Let's talk after breakfast." He mouthed: We may be bugged. Pierce nodded. Younger made him a substantial breakfast, and they chatted about the fine weather and lovely view. Then they went outside.

Younger led him down a trail to the beach, where

the surf thumped and hissed. They walked south, their feet sinking a little into the soft, wet sand.

"Something smells," Pierce said. He told Younger what he had learned.

"It's embarrassing to have a putsch here, of all places," Younger said when Pierce finished. "But it's not, mm, unheard of."

"We put down at least four or five a year. Most are just cultie revolts—death to the Antichrist, whatever. But this one is going to tear the Agency apart."

"But Gersen called the Agency in."

"He may have been afraid we'd eventually get wind of his plans. When suspected of a major crime, admit to a minor one. So he yelled sabotage and thought that might distract us until the putsch was ready."

"They must know they can't possibly win."

"No, they think they can. They think they have a gimmick, something we don't expect and can't counter. Presumably a WDS gimmick."

Younger stopped walking. "That means collusion with some of my people."

"Seamus Brown does play squash every week with Harry McGowan."

"Ah."

"I want Brown arrested, right away. And the Site must be sealed off for a day or two. Use just your own Security people, no Copos. Meanwhile, I'll get a message through your I-Screen to Wigner. The Agency will dump a battalion of Gurkhas on Farallon City to handle Gersen's Special Reserves."

They turned and began striding back along the beach. The sun threw their shadows across the advancing foam of the surf.

"Anything else?" Younger asked.

"I'd better talk to Anita !Kosi. She may know something about the gimmick."

"I'll call her right away." Younger nodded. Then he pitched forward onto the sand. Pierce saw the yellow tail of a flechette protruding from Younger's back and instantly dropped and began to roll. The shot aimed at him struck his left shoulder instead of his torso. The flechettes were loaded with a fast-acting paralytic drug: Pierce found he could still breathe, with effort, but could not move. He sprawled on his side, looking at Younger death-still a few paces away. A wave washed over Younger, but stopped before reaching Pierce. Withdrawing, the wave turned Younger over so he faced the sky. Younger's chest moved, very slowly.

Pierce heard distant footsteps. Two men, he decided, hurrying down the cliff through the brush. If they were far enough away, his body might be able to metabolize the drug before they reached him.

Another wave broke over Younger. With terrible slowness, he was rolled over again, his face resting underwater. Spray blew in Pierce's eyes, but he could not feel it.

After what seemed like a long time, two men in jeans and windbreakers trotted past him and out into the surf. They pulled Younger out of the water and dragged him up the beach. Pierce glimpsed their faces and recognized them as Special Reserve officers who had been part of the Secessionist group.

"Shit. He's dead."

"I was afraid of that. The old man's gonna freak. How 'bout the other one?"

One of them dug a toe under Pierce and flipped him onto his back. Pierce stared helplessly into the clear blue sky of a beautiful spring morning. He felt a few cramps in his hands and feet. The drug was wearing off.

The two men looked down at him. One of them, Pierce knew, was a man named Javier Ochoa; the other was Pablo Dietrich.

"Hello, Mr. Pierce," Ochoa said.

"Shoot him again—twice," Dietrich ordered. Ochoa, carrying a long-barreled Smith & Wesson .18, pointed it at Pierce's thigh. The rifle made two little puffing sounds, and Pierce's cramps vanished.

"Oughta hold him till next week," Ochoa grunted.

"No chance. See the way he started to duck? Fast.

He's been hyped. In half an hour he'll be good as new."

Suddenly Pierce was sitting up and watching the tracks his heels made in the sand as the two men dragged him along the beach. Getting back up the trail to Younger's house was slow work, and Pierce was almost glad he couldn't feel anything.

Ochoa and Dietrich dumped Pierce into an armchair in the living room, and left. Sitting on a couch in front of him, smoking a cigarette was Colonel Shih. He looked at Pierce dispassionately.

Time passed. Pierce heard a dragging noise: they were bringing Younger in. The two men reentered the living room and stood behind Pierce's chair, facing Shih.

"Cuff him." Shih's voice was a soft, unresonant tenor, but the men obeyed instantly and cuffed Pierce's wrists to the arms of his chair.

Shih focused at last on Pierce's eyes.

"How are you feeling?"

"Fair." His response came out as a spastic's croak, but at least his vocal cords were working again. His hands and feet hurt.

"I'm very sorry."

"Not at all."

"Do you understand what we have done?"

Pierce nodded.

"Can you tell me your understanding? I will correct you if necessary. But this is a time for frankness."

His mouth still felt thick and clumsy, but he could speak. "You ha' pa'bolic mikes on us—onna beash."

"Exactly."

"Di'creetly done."

"Thank you." A faint smile.

"You figured I'd seen th'oo sabotage sto'y, and wanted to check. When I said B'own had to be ar—arrested, you shot us."

"Why?"

"Sherlock—Sherlock is the gimmick. Or else the cover for the gimmick. I was supposed to clump around and get in people's hair for a few days. Till you were ready. But I twigged too soon." Pierce fell silent, starting breath exercises to dull the growing pain in his limbs.

"Much, much too soon. Now, tell me about your mission."

Pierce did so, including the fact that he had been blocked. Shih nodded and lit another cigarette, then whispered into his ringmike.

"Your block is alarming. It implies Dr. Wigner did not believe our story, and the implications of *that* are very serious." Shih smoked thoughtfully for a long minute. "You realize we shall have to Clear you. We must find out what went into your Briefing."

Pierce laughed. "Clear me? What's the point? You'd need Trainable technicians to monitor the Clearing, and it would take days—longer than you can afford."

Ochoa could not suppress a snort. Shih looked pained.

"Don't underestimate our resources, Mr. Pierce. We have Trainables who can accomplish it. In fact, they're preparing to do so up at our headquarters in Farallon City. Of course, they'll have to rush. I'm sorry, truly sorry. We wouldn't even consider such a step unless it were absolutely necessary."

"And it is."

"It is."

He was well and truly trapped. Short of some gross error by one or more of them, Pierce could see no way out. They would fly him back to Farallon City and unreel his mind like a ball of kite string in ten or twelve hours. Pierce almost looked forward to the exercise, for Training gave one a taste for strange and dangerous experiences. What would it be like to have his mind dissolved away, like a stain out of fabric? If he survived—was allowed to survive—he would have to learn absolutely everything all over again—how to suck, how to focus his eyes, how to repeat sounds and associate them with things and actions. Pierce had seen new minds grown on Cleared psychopaths; the new mind took longer to develop than the first and was rarely as good.

Shih snuffed out his cigarette and stood up. He was a slim man who carried himself with an aristocrat's easy erectness. "We'll have to carry you out in that chair, Mr. Pierce. I don't want you loose, but I don't want you drugged, either."

Ochoa spoke up with a total non sequitur: "Unlock his cuffs, sir? But—"

"Are you mad?" Shih interrupted. "I said no such thing."

"Well, okay, sir—if you've got him covered," Ochoa said. Then, before Dietrich could stop him, he freed Pierce's left hand and was moving behind the chair to unlock the other cuff.

"Stop him, Dietrich!"

Dietrich, standing on Pierce's left, drew a Mallory .15 and made the mistake of shooting Ochoa rather than Pierce. Pierce jumped up and swung the chair over his head, knocking Dietrich into the far wall. As the gun dropped, Pierce swept it up and fired once at Shih. Then he swung around to get Dietrich before the man could recover.

It was suddenly very quiet in Younger's house. Pierce found Ochoa's keys and unlocked the other cuff. Terribly tired, he collapsed back into the armchair facing Shih, who remained upright on the couch, mouth open, eyes blank. His chest rose and fell as slowly as Younger's had.

"I don't know how that happened," Pierce said hoarsely, "but I'm not sorry. You must be terribly disappointed."

He stood up and left the living room for a quick check of the house. As he had expected, Younger's Chloe lay dead in one of the bedrooms. She had been beaten and strangled. Pierce returned to the living room. He no longer felt tired; he felt very good.

"Colonel Shih, you're in trouble. You of all people ought to know how many capital offenses you've committed in the last hour. I think you'll talk to save yourself, though. So I'm taking you—" A name floated unbidden into his mind: Gordon Cole. "I'm taking you to a place where you can get an antidote for this nasty drug you use, and then we'll talk."

Shih stared past him, blankly. Pierce bent over Ochoa and broke the man's neck with a single sharp blow. Then he did the same to Dietrich.

"I'm sure you wish I'd call in Younger's Security people," Pierce said. "Then I might bog down in a homicide investigation while you told lies and stalled for time. Well, they'll learn of it, in a while. But first I'm going to peel you like an onion."

He carried Shih out to the Toyota and threw him into the back seat. Then he started back into town. An address, 127 Landau Street, occurred to him, and he realized it had to be Gordon Cole's. Pierce suddenly felt professional respect for Wigner's thoroughness.

A blue Datsun station wagon passed him, going the other way, but when Pierce checked the rearview mirror, he saw the car turning to follow him.

"Guess your reinforcements recognized me," he snapped at his passenger. "I'll have to lose them."

He did so most adroitly. But he knew that within minutes, Copo helicopters would be scanning every street in the city, despite the objections of Site Security. There was no way to ditch the car and proceed to Cole's on foot, not with a paralyzed man slung over his shoulder. There was nothing to do but barge in on Cole and hope that the man had the proper drugs with which to rouse and interrogate Shih. If the Copos moved in, Pierce would try to bring in Site Security; failing that, he would use Shih as a hostage. Failing *that*—he wished he knew more about Cole. Presumably he was an Agency stringer, supplying information to AID without actually being on the payroll.

In evading the Datsun, Pierce had spent fifteen minutes dodging up and down strange streets and back alleys. Now he headed straight for the East Side, a residential area. Most of the traffic was headed downtown at this time of day; even Trainable scientists kept peasants' hours.

Landau Street was lined with rambling white prefabs set on endless, identical lawns. Except for a few toddlers on trikes, the area was deserted. Number 127 seemed undistinguished: a broad, empty front lawn, the backyard screened by dense, high hedges, a strip of forest behind. The house itself was a low, sprawling box with curtained windows.

Pierce listened for helicopters, scanned the street, then slid smoothly out of the car. He pulled Shih out and carried him at a trot down to the front door.

Gordon Cole, a medium-sized man with red hair and green eyes, opened the door and helped Pierce lay Shih out on the floor of the spacious living room. Pierce had held on to the handcuffs and locked them on Shih's wrists, behind his back.

"He got a jolt about half an hour ago," Pierce said. "Got anything to wake him up, get him talking?" Shih lay on his side, gazing blankly at Pierce's feet.

"Sure."

"We need to work fast."

"I know."

In less than three minutes, Cole fired a hypospray into Shih's arm. Thirty seconds passed. Shih rolled onto his back, his eyes full of rage.

"Hi," Pierce called. "Now we're going to find out all about Project Sherlock."

Pierce heard a muffled bang under Shih's jacket. The man convulsed, once, and was dead. Pierce ripped off Shih's jacket and opened his shirt.

"Damn! A built-in self-destruct," he swore. The pseudoderm patch on Shih's chest had been blown away. Pierce saw a blackened hole between two ribs. As they watched, the hole filled with blood and the blood spread across the golden skin of Shih's chest. "Damn it. I should have checked."

"No reason to suspect anything like that," Cole replied, a little shakily. "I thought Agency people were the only ones that use 'em."

"I needed him very badly." Pierce grimaced. "The Copos will be here any minute."

"What's going on, anyway? You here to check out my report?"

"On—?"

"Gersen's misappropriation of funds, of course."

Pierce was puzzled. "I'll bite."

"Then why *are* you here?"

"Gersen sent us a memo about sabotage. Didn't you know?"

Cole laughed, a pleasantly boyish sound. "Bravo for Big Bengt. He must've known there was someone like me around, so he decided to muddy the waters."

"Your report wasn't part of my Briefing." Somehow Pierce was certain of that. "What was Gersen up to?"

"Creative accounting. He's switched over a billion dollars from various project budgets into Project Sherlock, all in the past month or so. But he's cooked the books to make them look as if Sherlock's budget was cut. Typical Colonial—he's ripped off most of the Colonial projects to do it. Somewhere in the process, someone has made a couple of hundred million. Really stupid, though—any Trainable could spot the discrepancies, no matter how nicely they're camouflaged. I notified Wigner a couple of weeks ago, but he didn't seem to respond. Until you dropped in, that is."

"It's more than that." Pierce quickly described what he had learned so far. Gordon Cole slouched into a hammock chair, listening so intently he did not notice when Shih's blood began to stain the carpet.

"Next move?" he asked.

"Notify Earth, somehow. McGowan will be guarding the I-Screens."

"I have one. A little message drop. Connects with the physics lab at UCLA on Earth. Using it will black out the whole neighborhood, though."

"The Copos will find us anyway. You might as well encode the message and pop it through. Then we'll disappear for a couple of days."

Abruptly, Pierce realized someone else was in the

house. An instant later he heard a voice behind him, a soft, musical voice that he recognized at once as that of Anita !Kosi:

"You must hurry, Gordon. The Copos are already closing in."

Pierce turned, smiled, and bowed. The woman was standing in a doorway that led to a long hall. She nodded absently. Her face was drawn.

"You're sure?" Cole asked.

"Absolutely. A patrol is coming through the woods behind the house, and a police jeep is down the street."

Cole frowned, perplexed. "How do you know?"

She was a small woman with peppercorn hair, skin the color of ripe apricots, and the face of a beautiful baby, but she lacked the belly and rump of a modern Bushman. Wearing a plain white sweater and faded jeans, she did not look impressive. Yet there was an absolute certainty in her voice, her folded arms, her immense dark eyes.

"I know." A glance at Pierce. "You are Jerry Pierce."

"Ma'am." He stood stiffly, feeling awkward as a doltish schoolboy. Holovision had conveyed her beauty, but not her dignity, nor her reserve. Anita !Kosi was not only a superb physicist, she was that twenty-first-century rarity, a great lady.

"I am here because I know Gordon works for Dr. Wigner."

Pierce glanced at Cole, who shrugged.

"When I became alarmed about Project Sherlock, I felt Wigner should be notified. Now we must act quickly. Gordon—tape a cassette and send it through to Earth at once."

"If they're already coming—?" Cole was agitated.

"Jerry and I will have to distract them."

"You can't. Too dangerous."

"I'll be in worse danger if they capture me without Wigner's learning of Sherlock and the putsch. Go on, quickly, and don't argue."

Cole silently obeyed, passing her in the doorway.

Anita looked down at Shih's corpse, then into Pierce's eyes. He realized that she was under a horrible strain.

"We've had a hard day together, you and I," she murmured.

Together? Pierce's puzzlement showed, but she did not explain.

"It's going to be even harder before we're finished," she continued. "We'll have to distract the Copos long enough for Gordon to get his message out. You're armed."

"Badly. This pistol's almost empty."

"We'll get you a better one. But I hope you won't have to use it."

She led him out of the house into the huge backyard. Some redwood patio furniture stood near a brick barbecue. The uncut grass stretched a hundred meters behind the house, where the woods began abruptly. Pierce could see men in camouflage uniforms moving through the trees with the quiet deliberation of professionals. They were coming toward the house.

"Let's sit down for a minute," Anita said.

Six:

The Copos' approach was hideously loud to Pierce's heightened hearing. He sat, legs crossed, in an uncomfortable deck chair. The Smith and Wesson's butt grew warm in his pocket as he held it. It was uncharacteristic of him to let anyone else take the lead in a fight, but Anita !Kosi evidently knew exactly what she was doing.

It became still. Without looking directly at the woods, Pierce could see the men—probably a full squad of ten—were searching for cover just inside the edge of the woods.

Suddenly he noticed a small commotion: thumps, cracklings. Pierce saw some of the Copos collapse.

"They're all out cold," Anita told him. "Quick—go grab a rifle from one of them."

He sprinted across the yard and into the trees. The nearest Copo was their sergeant, a huge Black man sprawled on his back. Pierce lifted the KG-15 rifle from the man's slack hand. The rifle was fully loaded with a clip of drugged flechettes, but the impact setting was a very lethal 10. A half-second burst from it would have blown Pierce and Anita to pieces. Pierce was about to dispatch the entire squad when he heard Anita call out a single word:

"*No.*"

He sighed and ran back across the yard. She was standing up, but seemed exhausted. When she spoke again, her voice was half-slurred.

"I couldn't stand ten deaths all at once."

"What the hell did you do to them?"

"Like Shih and his men—induced paralysis. They couldn't breathe, and passed out. But I can't . . . keep doing it. Need rest . . ."

Pierce heard a jeep rolling to a stop out near the front of the house. Dense shrubs stood between Cole's house and its neighbors. Pierce would have to slip through them in order to ambush the men in the street. He pulled Anita with him, and they crawled through until, by gently parting the branches, they could see out to the street.

The Toyota still stood at the curb, but its rear tires were flat. Fifty meters down the street, he could see a Copo armored jeep parked. Its windshield was down, and a rifle muzzle jutting over the hood was trained on Cole's front door. The jeep's radio buzzed and spluttered. Evidently the jeep's occupants had found the Toyota, disabled it, and then called for assistance. In moments, the area would be crawling with police.

"Can you do anything to those guys?"

She shook her head; her eyes were dull.

He cursed. "We need that jeep. Be ready to run when I bring it up the street."

She did not ask questions or argue. Pierce checked the clip, turned the impact setting to 4, stepped out of the bushes, and opened fire.

The Copos were much too slow to react. The KG-15 sprayed ten flechettes per second through the jeep's open windshield. The Copo rifle dropped with a clatter onto the hood.

Crouching low, Pierce raced across the broad, empty lawns to the jeep. He yanked open the driver's door. A young Copo toppled out, four flechettes imbedded in his face. His partner, the sniper, was also unconscious. Pierce considered stashing them in the Toyota. No time. Instead, he dragged both of them into the street and left them there, then jumped behind the wheel, lurched up to Cole's house, and slammed on the brakes. Anita ran out and climbed in. Pierce could hear the sibilant flutter of a helicopter overhead.

"What about Gordon?" Pierce asked, almost breath-
less.

"He's still encoding the message," she responded.

"Well, he'd better hurry. We're getting out of here."

With no real destination yet in mind, Pierce drove to
the next intersection and turned left. The jeep's windows were made of one-way glass; they passed several
Copos on foot, who waved casually as the jeep rolled
on by. A small dog chased them, barking furiously.

"They're in the house," Anita suddenly announced.

"Who?"

"The Copos. Gordon can hear them—pounding on
the door, the study door. The cassette's not ready, the
Screen isn't on . . . Oh. *OH!*"

She covered her face with her hands.

"What is it?"

"He's dead. Just like Shih. They must've gotten into
the room—Gordon knew he was caught—then a horrible pain in his chest, and nothing. He had a self-
destruct."

She began to cry, like a frightened child. Pierce kept
driving. He was scared and upset, but also somewhat
amused at himself. The most alarming aspect of this
business was the report he would have to write when it
was all over.

They reached the road out to Oppenheimer Field,
and Pierce swerved the jeep onto it. He switched on
the radio and listened for a minute to the chatter of
messages back and forth, about them. To add to the
Copos' confusion, he contributed a few false reports of
his own. He was a good mimic, and each report was
relayed in a different voice. Then, to avoid being
spotted by RDF, he switched off.

"We've got to get word back to Earth," Anita said
unsteadily.

"All the I-Screens will be guarded. Gersen might
even shut down all traffic, just to make sure we don't
send someone else through." He smiled wryly. "Not
that we have much to tell. Wigner will want some hard
facts before he sends in the Gurkhas."

"Perhaps we can get something at Mojave Verde. Some of my colleagues are still working on Sherlock—"

"No. We're going to Farallon City."

"What? But there's no time—"

"We just have to. I've got to get to Gersen." He knew for sure now that he had to kill Gersen; whatever Sherlock might turn out to be, Gersen's death would stall it. "Trust me, ma'am. I know what I'm doing."

He turned on the radio again, this time to a regular broadcast wavelength.

"—repeat, Dr. Eugene Younger, Director of the Weapons Development Site, was murdered early this morning by an employee of the Agency for Intertemporal Development named Gerald Pierce. Colonial Police spokespersons say they have no motive for the brutal slaying, but expect to arrest Pierce at any moment. He is believed to be somewhere in Los Alamitos and should be considered armed and extremely dangerous. Police describe him as a white male, mid-thirties, height about one hundred eighty centimeters, weight seventy-five to eighty kilos, short brown hair, cleanshaven, last seen wearing a brown duffel coat. Anyone seeing a man meeting this description is urged to contact Colonial Police headquarters. We repeat—"

They were nearly at the airfield, driving fast on the deserted road. As they rounded a curve, Pierce saw a black Ford sedan parked on the opposite shoulder, facing them. A man, obviously a plainclothes Copo, stepped out of the sedan, raised an old-fashioned bullet-firing .45. Steadying himself against the car door and holding the pistol in both big hands, the Copo fired. The windshield cracked loudly, but held. Pierce steered straight for the man, accelerating.

"*Don't kill him!*"

"I won't." But even as the Copo dived over the hood of the sedan, and the jeep skidded back into its own lane, Pierce realized he *could* not—after that command—have killed the man. He glanced at Anita, and met her gaze. There was an excruciating pain in her eyes, and grief; but there was also a power in them to which only an idiot would not defer.

The gateway to Oppenheimer Field had been shut. As they approached, three Copos fired on them through the gate's wire mesh, to no effect.

"Hang on," Pierce ordered, and they crashed through the gate. Flechettes spattered on the windows like bugs. A field attendant, with more courage than brains, drove a baggage train across the jeep's path, and Pierce narrowly missed him. Then they were out on the main runway, racing for a row of hangars.

The first hangar was empty; the second held a medium-range Mitsubishi M120 with its starboard engine dismantled. In the third hangar stood a Cessna C60. Pierce drove right inside under its wing and jumped out. The smell of jet fuel was pleasantly strong.

Three men in ground-crew coveralls were standing near the hangar's rear wall, staring out over their coffee mugs. They were well away from anything that might be a weapon, but Pierce was taking no chances and shot all three at low impact. They cried out, more in fear than in pain, then collapsed.

"Pull out the chocks," he called to Anita. As she did so, he sprang up the gangway and into the Cessna's tiny cabin. A sour-faced technician was rising from the pilot's seat as Pierce shot her. The seconds ticked away in his mind as he carried her out. It seemed to take a long time before he and Anita were in the cockpit—alone.

She helped him through a hasty preflight checkout, and he started the engines. The Cessna taxied out into the noon sunshine; Pierce steered for the nearest runway. He glanced over at the terminal building. A small crowd had gathered on the observation deck. No doubt quite an uproar was taking place behind the green glass of the control-tower windows. But there were no Copos visible. Pierce studied the white bulb of the radome, which gave the control tower an oddly Russian look. Then he pointed the Cessna down the runway and poured on power. They were in the air very quickly.

"We've made it!" Anita sighed, relieved.

"Not quite. Not yet." He put them into a steep climb as he mentally reviewed everything he knew about the plane he was flying. It was a tough, reliable subsonic, designed for short-range flights and sensible pilots. He was about to stress it badly.

They climbed west, out over the coast, until they reached an altitude of two thousand meters and began to circle. Los Alamitos looked very small, a little geometric space carved out of a green-and-beige wilderness. There was considerable traffic below on the road to Oppenheimer Field, and Pierce could see the regular fluttering glint of a helicopter's rotors as it circled the terminal building. The radome stood out vividly. Pierce tilted the Cessna's nose down and put on power. Anita seemed nervous.

"I've got to blind them," he explained.

Their dive steepened as they accelerated, and the field grew larger again. The helicopter hovered near the terminal, evidently preparing to land. It was a Copo craft.

Anita understood what he planned, and rested a hand on his arm. "Please—some will be killed."

"Stop me, then, and *we'll* be killed."

She made no response.

The plane had passed the speed of sound as it swept within two hundred meters of the control tower. The shock wave shattered the radome, blew in the control-tower windows, and knocked the helicopter off balance. It slammed into the asphalt and burst into flame.

Pierce regained just enough altitude to bring them over the Santa Monica Mountains. The nearest aircraft that could track or catch them were the fighters based at Mojave Verde. By the time they could be alerted, the Cessna would be long gone. He began to relax.

"In real life I'm a mild-mannered reporter for the *New Orc Times*." He grinned and looked over at Anita. Her face was a nightmare mask of agony.

"Get away, shut them out, get away, get away, they're dying so slowly—"

Pierce felt his self-congratulation turn sour. He had to protect this woman, but doing so half destroyed her. They flew on in silence for a few minutes, until she gradually relaxed.

"You'd better tell me more of what's going on," he finally said.

"Oh, shut up." She reached out blindly and grasped his hand. Her breathing was harsh. "I'm sorry. I feel better now. They're out of range. Poor people. Poor suffering people!"

"You seem to be some kind of telepath."

"A clumsy word. It's less than that—and more. I can sense emotions, kinesthesia—especially strong feelings in people I know. And, as you've found out, I can influence others."

"By some kind of direct stimulation of their nervous systems."

"Yes. I did it with Shih and his men. And with the Copos in the forest. But projecting is hard. So hard." She looked half drugged; her eyes were heavy-lidded, her voice slurred. "I can't do any more. Not for a day or two. Need rest."

"But you can still receive?"

"Mm. Yes, oh, yes. We never lose that. Sometimes it's like—like having your eyes taped open in a room full of spotlights."

"*We?* Others can do this as well?"

"All of us. Everyone in the family."

"The psychologists must know."

"No. We agreed at the very beginning to keep that much secret."

Pierce laughed without amusement. "Concealing anything from them is a better trick than reading minds. You realize such a talent can't be kept secret any longer? I'll have to inform the Agency. It's too important."

"Well, we'll see."

Pierce had an unpleasant suspicion: she might be able to erase his knowledge of her abilities, and might well do so if she could work out a plausible cover story. Well, he had enough to worry about.

"You really are the people of the future, aren't you?"

"Oh my. We've tried so hard to live that down." Pierce recalled that when the !Kosis had first been discovered in South Africa on Luvah, they had been identified as Boskopoids, ancestors of the modern Bushmen. Someone had remembered an old essay by an American anthropologist named Eiseley, who had pointed out how closely the Boskopoids had resembled the stereotype of future mankind: big-brained, small-bodied, baby-faced people. The !Kosis' talents had strengthened the idea. Their IQs were unmeasurably high; they were all Trainables, even the adults. Pierce was beginning to suspect that the Testing teams had probably been manipulated by the !Kosis, since adults were normally never even considered for Testing. For a year or two the popular media had been full of articles about the Boskopoids as Homo superior, despite the unarguable fact that they had died out as a distinct group on all chronoplanes uptime from Luvah.

"No it's true," Pierce insisted. "You're the next step up from us. Your brains, your talents—"

"If you were an educated man, and not merely a Trained one, you wouldn't say that. There's no progress in evolution, only response to change. We're just a mutant strain, and our mutations lead nowhere."

Pierce looked confused.

"Our talents, as you call them, are a curse. You've seen what it does to me to be near a wounded or dying person. It's almost more than one can bear. We can even share the feelings of animals—that's why we were grubbers of roots when your people found us. For us, even birth is terrible. The whole family shares the mother's pain—mother and baby share each other's pain. We share our joys, too, and they're very great, but our sorrows . . ."

They flew in silence for a time, north on an irregular zigzag course into San Joaquin Valley.

"So you knew all about us, right from the first contact with the Testing and Recruiting teams."

"Sooner. We were aware of them a few days before that first visit. In fact, we followed the team. We shared their feelings, looked at our world through their eyes. It's hard to describe. But we *knew* them, we knew what they were looking for, and we knew somehow that we had what they wanted. Then we went away from them, to decide what to do. We went to one of our holy places, a little lake by the Orange River. We thought our gods would tell us what to do. Instead, the holy place seemed just a deserted little lake, and nothing more. The rock paintings we had made there seemed stupid and childish, not sacred."

She paused for a moment. "We were so wretched. Our world didn't mean anything to us, any more, so we had to come to yours." Her voice turned cold and bitter. "And among the many things we've learned since then, we've learned that our sensitivity will vanish in the end and that our descendants will be the luckier for it."

"Not now. The Boskopoids on the other chronoplanes died out, but you and your family have managed to escape."

"The same thing will happen to us, in a century or two. There's too much pain and death, Jerry; we can't escape it. We can only conceal its effects on us by deluding others or robbing them of their memories. You're not the first person to learn our secrets."

Pierce's earlier suspicion was confirmed. Now he might as well learn as much as he can. "How far can you send and receive?"

"The distance varies. Perhaps ten kilometers, with someone I know. Two or three with someone I don't."

"How did you get into contact with Shih and his men? Did you know them?"

No, but I knew Chloe and Eugene. I felt her death, like hearing a scream, and then his."

"You were staying with Gordon Cole?"

"Since yesterday. I knew he was working for the

Agency, and he seemed to expect something important to happen. When he invited me to stay with him, I knew he was afraid I might be hurt if I didn't."

"He knew about your abilities?"

"I told him a little, when I had to."

Pierce found a chocolate bar in his coat pocket, and shared it with her. "You complicate matters very interestingly." He smiled. "Gersen has a program; Wigner has a program. But neither program takes you into account. That makes it all more fun."

"Fun! You see me as a means of helping you kill Gersen, and you call that fun."

Damn the woman, and damn himself for his schoolboy's veneration of her! She was not yet twenty-two, but she somehow mantled herself in a queen's reserve. Well, he would have to serve her, even if it meant bullying her.

"Of course it's fun. It might as well be, since I've got to kill him in any case, and enjoying the deed will help me succeed."

"You've *got* to do it?"

He explained his blocked Briefing, his desire to kill Gersen, Shih, and McGowan at the Farallon City airport. "Wigner knows enough about Project Sherlock to want it stopped. I'm just executing his orders."

"Whatever they may be."

"Whatever they may be."

Anita became silent. Five kilometers below, the brown fields of spring rolled by under broken clouds. On the eastern horizon, the white teeth of the Sierra Madre glittered against the sky.

"But the project is impossible."

Pierce looked at her.

"The technology is beyond us. To create a usable magnetic lens, the generators must be perfectly aligned—perfectly. A discrepancy of twenty-five meters—between generators millions of kilometers apart—would mean the mother ship, the receiver, would get a hopeless mess. We're nowhere near that sort of precision."

"Yet you kept pushing the project."

"Until I saw how serious the problems were. I wouldn't have let Seamus Brown take me off Sherlock if I'd felt we were close to a solution. But I missed something," she went on, "something about it that makes it a weapon." She shrugged. "I feel worse about being stupid than about being chased by the Copos."

"Well. Whatever Sherlock may be, neutralizing Gersen should stop it."

"You're very confident."

"Of course."

"And how will you . . . neutralize him?"

"That will be determined by circumstances, and my Briefing."

Anita looked over at him. He forced himself to meet her eyes. She embarrassed him, made him feel like a teenager caught playing cops-and-robbers when he should have outgrown such games. Under this embarrassment he resented her. Who was *she* to question his mission? She was a kind of superhuman, but she might also become a hindrance.

If that chain of thought had additional links, he was unaware of them. He began the descent to Nuevo Sacramento.

Seven:

Pierce gave Nuevo Sacramento's Air Traffic Control a false identification and received permission to land. He taxied the Cessna right to the terminal building. They jumped out and walked quickly inside. At this latitude, away from the coast, winters were long, so even on this sunny April afternoon there was a chill in the air.

The terminal was not very crowded, and no one took much notice of them as they walked on through. A young Copo stood by the doors to the road, watching them approach. He moved to intercept them, but his relaxed expression indicated that this was only a routine check.

"Excuse me, sir—ma'am. May I see your IDs, if you don't mind?"

"Of course." Pierce showed his intertemporal passport. The Copo's eyebrows lifted a little, but his manner did not warm from civility to courtesy. He did not seem to recognize in Pierce anything but a senior bureaucrat from Earth.

"Welcome to Nuevo, Mr. Pierce. Hope you have a nice visit. Sure picked a good day. And your ID, ma'am?"

"I haven't any. It's really annoying. All my cards were lost this morning, and I can't think where I left them."

The Copo looked concerned. "Sorry to hear that, ma'am. If you can't produce your ID, I'll have to ask you to come in to our office for fingerprinting. Just a formality, you understand. Then we can issue you a temporary ID for your visit here."

A cab pulled up outside, and a frumpy young couple shuffled in. The cab stayed at the curb, its driver immersed in a carno comic.

"I'm sorry," said Pierce, "but we're really pressed for time. We'll be here just for a couple of hours—then we're off again back to Little St. Louis."

"Well, sir, I'm afraid I don't make the regulations. Now, if you'll come this way—" He gestured down the long concourse to an unmarked door. Pierce reached out, gripped the man's outstretched wrist, and flung him off balance. The Copo hit the floor head first, his mouth and nose spraying blood across the gray vinyl floor.

Anita gasped and began to sag, until Pierce grasped her shoulders and guided her smoothly through the doors. Rapid footsteps sounded behind them—bystanders going to the Copo's aid.

They were outside, half running across the sidewalk to the cab. The driver lifted his sallow face from his comic and gaped at the muzzle of Pierce's pistol.

"Hey, whatcha doin'?"

"Out."

"Hey, watcha doin'?"

"Out of the cab—*now*."

"Huh?"

"Oh, hell." Pierce shot him on low impact and opened the door. The driver, eyes rolled up in his head, fell heavily onto the oily asphalt. Anita got in and slid over to make room for Pierce behind the wheel. He started the engine and pulled sedately away from the curb. The driver lay face up on the road, his comic fluttering beside him.

"Sorry I had to be so rough," Pierce said.

"Yes, yes. Never mind." She stared at the dashboard. "I've never been this weak before. I tried to stop the Copo—really tried. And nothing. And I couldn't stop them killing Gordon. It's like being paralyzed."

"Nothing could have saved Gordon."

"If I could have stopped the Copos from breaking in, he'd at least have lived to get the message out."

Glancing across at her, Pierce saw she was on the edge of a real breakdown. He tried, and failed, to imagine what it must be like to be a !Kosi. They all were gentle people, scholars and thinkers as isolated in their new world as they had been in their old one. Now he was escorting her through a very dangerous passage. If she were hurt or killed, the repercussions would be immense.

"Do a mantra. Rest," he told her. She nodded and closed her eyes; in a few seconds she grew calmer.

They turned west onto Highway 605, headed for Nuevo Sacramento. There was little traffic at this time of day, except for some trucks and the occasional bracero bus carrying migrant workers. Pierce monitored the cab's CB radio, but heard nothing unusual. In a few minutes there would surely be an all-points bulletin out on them. They would have little chance of getting through Nuevo Sacramento undetected, let alone of reaching Farallon City.

Already they were on the ragged edge of town, a patchwork of marshes, truck farms, housing tracts, and light industry. There seemed to be an abandoned car in every front yard; grubby kids with slingshots sniped at them from the side of the road. Colonials.

"There's a shopping center over by the next off-ramp," Pierce said. "We'll ditch the cab there."

They left it in the crowded parking lot and ambled into the covered shopping mall. Built in a classic 1960s style, it resembled a thousand others on a dozen chronoplanes, right down to the aimless teenagers dawdling outside the shoe boutiques and pornotheques. Pierce and Anita walked into the giant department store at one end of the mall; he was glad to see it was a sale day, and the store was crowded with haggard housepersons and their squalling children. The store affected an old-fashioned decor, complete with a pseudo-wooden floor; most of the merchandise was shabby and over-priced junk from Earth.

"Let's buy some new clothes," he suggested, and gave her a couple of hundred-dollar bills. Using a credit card would surely give them away to the databank computers, which by now must be programmed with all their documents. UnTrainables being old-fashioned about sex roles as well as about merchandising, there were separate men's and women's clothing departments, complete with changing rooms. Pierce felt rather silly observing such niceties. No wonder they needed pornotheques!

He bought khaki trousers, a red-and-black-checked flannel shirt, serviceable Swiss hiking boots, an olive-drab jacket, and a black baseball cap. The clothes all looked too new, but at least he now blended in with most of the other males.

Anita met him back on the mall. Her jeans and sweater had been replaced by ugly red-and-green overalls, a red turtleneck sweater, and a black windbreaker. She wore a short Afro wig, and a chromofilm spray had turned her golden skin a rich brown. The chromofilm would break down in a few hours, but right now it made her considerably less conspicuous. When Pierce slouched up beside her, they looked like a typical Colonial farm couple, in town for an afternoon's shopping.

"There's a Copo car in the parking lot," Anita murmured. "They must have spotted the cab."

"Okay. Back into the store."

They sidled through the crowds, found a stairway to the basement, and took it. No one was visible in the basement, but mariachi music bleated from a radio somewhere nearby. They slipped silently through a labyrinth of shelves and cartons. It was lunchtime; no one was around.

An open door led to a loading dock facing a parking area. Pierce considered stealing one of the three trucks standing there unattended, but decided against doing so—the alarm would go out within minutes, and the trucks were too easily identifiable. Beyond the parking area, trees screened this side of the building from the highway. They would have to take their chances on the road.

No one saw them cross the lot and then the highway. There was a hitchhikers' shelter on the shoulder of the westbound side, and Pierce and Anita stood beside it, thumbs out. Four or five cars hissed by, including an unmarked Copo Toyota, whose driver regarded them indifferently. More police would be in the area soon.

A bracero bus groaned down upon them. Its yellow paint was camouflaged under a thick crust of dirt, and its dented front bumper carried a Spanish title: EL EMPERADOR SIN ROPA. It stopped. The driver was a heavy, apathetic man, clearly no more than the chauffeur for the woman beside him. She rolled down the window and stared at them through mirrored sunglasses. Strands of gray-blond hair had escaped from under her old straw hat. She wore a brown wool jacket; her hand, resting on the window frame, was gloved.

"Hi," she said. "You folks lookin' for a ride, or for work?"

"Both." Pierce smiled.

"You wearin' nice clothes for people need work."

Pierce shrugged and grinned. "Well, yes, ma'am. Just bought 'em. Now we just about broke."

"Is that right. You ain't runaway indents?"

"No, ma'am! Free agents." He considered drawing his pistol and commandeering the bus, but two more police cars were coming down the highway. Pierce saw no occasion for dramatics; all they needed, after all, was a ride out of town.

"Well, you better be. I find an indent, he goes back to his boss by special delivery."

"Yes, ma'am."

"Go climb in the back with the others." She turned, slid open a panel between the cab and the back of the bus. "Dallow! Got a couple more comin' in. You let 'em in. Get 'em settled."

"You bet, Miz Curtice," a young man's voice replied. There was some fuss and muttering from the unseen passengers; Mrs. Curtice silenced it by slamming the panel shut.

"Hurry up," she told them.

"Mighty obliged, ma'am." Pierce smiled again.

They walked to the rear of the windowless bus, where the door was already open for them. Anita paused.

"Something's wrong."

"Don't worry. In you go." He followed her into the dim interior of the bus.

—And was knocked sprawling to the cold metal floor. Stunned, he heard the door slam, felt the bus lurch into motion. He was already beginning to recover, to tense for a lashing kick out at his assailant, when hands fumbled at his left wrist.

Very far away, he heard Anita screaming. He was not sure how long she had been screaming; he only knew that he himself had been in agony forever. Somewhere back at the beginning of his life, someone had hit him, and then, a moment later, his hand had been—shot off? burned? crushed? Pierce wasn't sure, and it never occurred to him to open his eyes and look.

The pain stopped. At least, the agony in his wrist stopped; it took some time for the convulsed muscles in his arm and shoulder to recover. He lay quietly on the floor, doing his breathing exercises automatically. His new clothes were drenched with sweat. Someone frisked him, took his pistol.

"Least you ain't no crybaby." It was the young man, Dallow. "And you pack some solemn armament. Here, pass this piece up to Miz Curtice . . . Okay, c'mon, sit up." He was pulled onto one of two broad benches running the length of the bus.

Pierce saw a white plastic band around his wrist. An inductance bracelet, of course. And handled by a real pro. There was no point in trying to break it—the plastic was too tough. He looked around.

The bus was crowded with adults and children, a

typical assortment of indentured workers: Sicilians, Mexicans, Egyptians, Portuguese, some American Blacks. They all wore the bracelets. A few grinned at him, grateful for the entertainment he and Anita had provided. The bus stank of old sweat and fresh urine.

Pierce found himself sitting next to a lean, under-sized young Black with a gap-toothed smile and intelligent, crazy eyes. He held a half-meter truncheon with the authority of a field marshal.

"How you head, man?"

"Hurts."

"You got some thick head, man. You the first I ever see start to get up after I hit 'em."

Pierce stood, a little unsteadily, and lifted Anita from the floor. When he held her in his lap, she slumped against him like a sleeping baby.

"Watchoo name, man?"

"Jerry."

"Watchoo woman name?"

"Anita. What's yours?"

The young man shifted the truncheon to his left hand and extended his right. Around the wrist was a fluorescent orange ID strap, wider than the inductance bracelet on the other wrist. Pierce read the strap:

DALLOW, WM. C.
Indent. # 0-671-5512
Expiry Date: 1 Jan 20
Property of: Curtice Labor Brokers
702 E. Eisenhower Avenue
Nuevo Sacramento, Orc
Phone: (603) 771-1654

"Call me Dallow. And don't give me no shit. I'm Miz Curtice's chief honcho an'ass kicker. You get along with me, you gonna get along with her and that little wand she got."

Pierce nodded. Anita stirred; Dallow touched her head to see how hard she had been hit, and dislodged her wig. Even in the dim light, her orange skin and peppercorn hair looked strange. Dallow was alarmed; so were the other workers close enough to see.

"What's all this, man? She sick or somethin'? She got funny hair."

"Nothing's wrong with her. She's using chromofilm. Her skin's the same color as her scalp."

"No shit. She got some disease?" Colonials lived in dread of local germs.

"None."

"Watchee want to look Black, then?"

"We didn't want to make it easy for the cops."

"Hunh. What they want with you?"

"I shot a couple of 'em."

"Hunh. Man, you shot 'em good. Har'ly any ammo left in that piece I took off of you." He thought for a moment. "We ain't no special friends of the *po*lice. You do what I tell you, you smooth with us."

"Good." Pierce was annoyed at this development. But the bus was moving west toward Farallon City, and that was the important thing. "We'll cooperate."

Dallow whooped. "Man, we *all* cooperate with Miz Curtice! Nobody like a taste of bracelet, they can avoid it. 'Sides, she a smooth lady. She got some style."

"How'd you meet her?" Pierce asked.

"Hunh. Like most of these dopies—got my ass kicked downtime to this shithole. They lay on all that good shit, everybody get a job down here, hunh? Sure. Lotta guys like me, they go endo, live in some cave somewheres. Hunh! Some never-never. So I get indented, okay? Least you gets paid steady, work or no work. An' Miz Curtice, she make sure you work. Food in the camps ain't so smooth, but—" He shrugged good-naturedly.

"Indents don't wear bracelets."

"Yeah, well, hunh. You broker sell you contrac', you go where you told. Miz Curtice, she a blackbirder arright, but she smooth, she better'n most. Can't blame her. Lots indents goes AWOL 'less they got a bracelet. You go AWOL and get picked up, you in *bad* shape, you *wish* you have a bracelet. Getchoo ass pounded good, and then they don' pick up you option, man. You starvin'. Miz Curtice, she make sure her people don't get themself in that fix."

"What about the Copos? Blackbirding's illegal."

"Aw, they smooth, they unnerstan'. What they s'posed to do, bust all the blackbirders? Then we all on the road AWOL again, makin' trouble for everybody. Shit, the Copos got enough trouble without messin' with us."

Anita gasped and woke in tears. Pierce cradled her gently and whispered to her in first-century Greek: "All is well, all is well, these people will not harm us." His words sounded more comforting, somehow, in that formal and archaic tongue.

"My arm hurts," she whimpered in English. Then, in Greek: "My arm hurts. Where are we?"

"Whatsat you sayin'?" Dallow growled.

"She's an African," Pierce said. "She likes to talk in Swahili; she taught me how."

"Hunh. Ex*treme*. She teach me? You teach me Swahili, sister?"

"Oh—yes, brother."

"Arright." But Dallow was in no hurry to learn; calmed by knowing that they conversed in an acceptable language, he relaxed and ignored them. The others watched for a while, then withdrew into their own gossip or private fantasies.

"We have been taken captive," Pierce said. "The woman in the cab is a—*melanorthis*? A slave owner. She's bound for the coast."

Anita looked revolted. "What can we do?"

"For now, nothing. At least we're headed in the right direction."

"You tolerate enslavement for the sake of your mission?"

"This is not really enslavement. Where struggle is futile, acceptance is wisdom."

"So self-deception often calls itself."

He said nothing. First-century Greek, he reflected, could sting as well as comfort.

The bus crawled slowly west through the afternoon, stopping only infrequently. During those breaks Dallow watched everyone closely, including the women squatting behind trees.

"Ev'body wanna get in some AWOL time," he commented to Pierce. "Shit, I gone AWOL plenny. But Miz Curtice don't go for that, unh-unh. She like to show up *on* time, *in* place, with *ev'*body 'counted for. Thataway you gets a good rep with the bosses . . . *O*kay, people, le's go, shake it more'n twice you playin' with it!"

"D'you know where we're headed?" Pierce asked as everyone drifted back to the bus.

"We know when we get there. Miz Curtice don' tell us nothin' till we need to know it."

Pierce and Anita were about to climb back in the bus when Mrs. Curtice called them over.

"What's the matter with your skin, girl? You got a disease?"

"No—it's just chromofilm."

"You call me ma'am."

"Yes, ma'am."

"I know it's chromofilm, I got eyes. I mean underneath." The film had already begun to fleck off Anita's cheeks and throat. "You got jaundice or something?"

"That's my natural skin color—ma'am."

"Is that right. What are you, some kinda Jap-nigger cross?"

She hesitated. "That's right, ma'am."

"Thought so. I can usually tell." She turned to Pierce. "You come with me, I wanna talk to you. But keep your distance."

The bus was parked in a muddy clearing just off the highway; judging by the litter and stink of excrement, it was a regular stop for bracero buses. Mrs. Curtice and Pierce walked slowly around the edge of the clearing, watching where they put their feet. She moved stiffly, and Pierce realized with surprise that she had arthritis and was in considerable pain.

"You didn't buy those clothes, did you?"

"No, ma'am. Anita found this credit card in the ladies' changing room—in the department store? So we figured we might as well use it to get some new clothes. But the card musta been reported, 'cause they nearly nailed us."

"Is that right?"

"Yes, ma'am."

"You can cut the horseshit, bud. You aren't no glorified shoplifter, not packing a goddam Smith and Wesson. And that Jap-nigger girlfriend of yours is so straight I'd like to kick her fat ass." She winced as she stepped over a log.

"Would you like to stop and rest, Mrs. Curtice?"

"No, I would not. Don't change the subject. You're some kind of professional, right?"

"Uh—I won't deny it, ma'am."

"Thought so. You prob'ly work for one of them spic gangsters down in Mexicopolis. You sure as hell ain't a Copo. So what the hell you doin', hitchin' rides on 605 with that funny-lookin' kid?"

"Ma'am, believe me when I tell you with all due respect that it's a lot safer for you if you don't know anything about us."

"Is that right. And maybe it's a lot safer for *you*." She paused breathing hard. "Copos like to get their paws on you, I bet. Might even be a reward in it."

Pierce said nothing.

"But I pay off the Copos every month; no need to give 'em something extra 'less I need to. Want to get that strap off your wrist?"

"Yes, ma'am."

"You've killed people."

"I have."

"Knew it the second I clapped eyes on you. You got than clean-cut crazy look. You kill somebody for me, I let you and your girlfriend go."

"Who's the candidate?"

"A blackbirder on Luvah. Lives in New Monterey, runs a chain of pornotheques with indent girls."

"Well, ma'am, I'd be glad to oblige, but I can't get through an I-Screen without papers."

"I know a knotholer in Little Frisco. Fat little kraut named Klein. He'll send you through."

"Suppose I just went through and disappeared?"

"Suppose you did. We'd sure give your girlfriend one fine working over 'fore we gave her to the Copos. And we'd tip 'em off about you as well, so you wouldn't last very long . . . Deal?"

"It's a deal." He had no intention of doing Mrs. Curtice's chores for her; he intended to go nowhere but Farallon City and to kill no one but Gersen and McGowan. But he had to oblige Mrs. Curtice until he could get that wand out of her grip. "When do you want this done?"

"Tomorrow. You go through, drive down to New Monterey, and come right back again. This time tomorrow, you and your friend are on your way."

"This knotholer—can you trust him?"

"Sure." Her legs were hurting her. "He knows his stuff. I've used him four, five times. Bastard charges plenty, but he's good. Why, you scared of going through a knothole?"

"Well—"

"Nothin' to be ashamed of. We're all scared of somethin'. But Klein's got good equipment and he knows how to run it. Know what scares me?"

"Ma'am?"

"Drugs. Head drugs. Worst thing you can ever do to yourself is let yourself take anything that works on your mind. I don't care what, grass, speed, enkephalin, DDG. Rather drop dead than let some goddamn blinkie doctor shoot me full of that crap. They make you think they're doin' you a favor—next thing you know, you're doin' *them* the favors, and you don't even know it. Unh-unh."

They returned to the bus, Mrs. Curtice walking slowly through her pain.

It was early evening when they pulled into a migrant workers' camp in the Alcatraz Valley. Dallow and a few others were detailed to pick up supper at the camp's mess hall; Mrs. Curtice silently oversaw the conversion of the bus into a dormitory. Boards were laid across the aisle between the benches; hammocks were slung, bedrolls brought out, the toilet hooked up to the camp sewer. The meal, when it arrived was something resembling chop suey, spooned out of plastic buckets and eaten at battered picnic tables. Other groups, screened by scrub alder but very audible, were camped nearby.

"How are you feeling?" Pierce asked Anita as they shared their supper.

"I'm freezing, but I'm not as upset as I was."

"Good." He watched the children as they ran through the blue twilight, screaming exuberantly. "Just treat this as some kind of horrible holiday. We'll be out of here in a day—two at the outside."

Mrs. Curtice walked slowly up to them.

"Stand up when I approach you."

They obeyed.

"How you gettin' on? Food okay?"

"Yes, ma'am," said Pierce.

"Good. I look after my people, they look after me. You Americans?"

"Yes, ma'am."

"Figured you was. Still got some spunk and brains. These goddamn greaseballs can't zip their flies without me tellin' 'em how. No responsibility. No initiative. 'Patron-dependent groups,' they call 'em. Kids are the worst. The old folks used to work, anyway—they remember how to look busy. Guess how old I am."

"Ma'am, I really couldn't."

"Sixty. No shit. And I can whip every ass in this outfit, arthritis or not. Sixty."

"Hard to believe," Pierce said politely.

"Believe it or not, I saw Nixon get shot in '63. I was eight, goin' on nine, the toughest little bitch in Texas. Never forget that day. My daddy always said that was the end of the good times. Now you look at these young clowns, shit! They never heard of Nixon."

"Uh, you mean Kennedy, don't you, ma'am?"

"Kennedy, Nixon, whoever." She shrugged. "Yeah—Nixon resigned or something, didn't he? See, that's what I mean—it was all downhill after '63. Look at America now, takin' orders from greaseballs in the IF, shippin' good citizens downtime to make room for endo blinkies. It's a goddamn plot, you ask me. The same people that got ridda Nixon and Kennedy. It's all a goddamn plot." She shifted her weight. "Well, let's get these people bedded down. Big day tomorrow." She grinned unpleasantly at Pierce.

Everyone was locked inside the bus. Pierce found himself cramped between Dallow and Anita. "Where does Mrs. Curtice sleep?" he asked.

"She got a little bunk above the cab. Now shuddup and go to sleep—we make too much noise, she give us all a tingle."

"Dallow—" His voice was a murmur. "How'd you like to be a rich, rich man? Have anything you want?"

"Like it fine."

"We can make you a rich man, Dallow. You could have a big car, a house, your own servants if you want 'em."

"Unh-hunh. Sure. What I gotta do for all this?"

"Help us get that damn wand away from Mrs. Curtice. That's all."

Dallow snorted softly in the smelly darkness. "Man, you mus' think I dumb. What I want to hassle her for, just 'cause you make big promises?" He turned over, and went to sleep almost at once.

"Always trying," Anita whispered in Greek. "Never mind. By the morning I should have my powers back." She paused. "I wish she would go to sleep—her pain makes me uncomfortable. And her anxiety."

"What are you talking about?"

"She is always a little afraid. And there is an—anticipation in her. Not pleasant. It must be about the job she wants you to do. I suppose your regular employers must feel something similar when they send you out on a job."

"Mmm." He rolled over, so that they lay back to back. "Sleep well. This time tomorrow, the whole plan will be stymied."

Despite Mrs. Curtice's liking for quiet, the bus was noisy—children whined, people joked, quarreled, made love. Anita turned and snuggled against him.

"All the fornication makes me amorous." Her small, smooth hand slipped inside his shirt and did a gentle *effleurage* across his chest.

"No."

"As you wish." Her lips brushed his ear as she whispered: "When I regain my powers, I'll give you a permanent erection, like a !Kosi man, and then I'll do things to your senses that the psychologists never dreamed of." She giggled like a little girl.

"Good night. Go to sleep." He masked his anxiety with enough brusqueness to deceive himself that he was not interested. He began the breathing exercises that would put him to sleep in thirty seconds; just before they worked, he felt her hand move down his ribs, pause a moment, and then withdraw. He fell into a troubled sleep.

Eight:

Next morning, Pierce had been awake for a long time when the rear door was unlocked and gray light seeped in.

"Pierce," Mrs. Curtice said quietly. He felt a light tingle on his wrist, rose, and stepped over Dallow, who blinked up at him.

Mrs. Curtice hobbled to one of the picnic benches and slowly seated herself, ignoring the heavy dew. Pierce stood seven or eight meters away from her.

"Christ, it really hurts this morning. Anyway. We're goin' to town today, you an' me, and you're gonna go through Klein's knothole."

"Ma'am."

"Here's the drill." She gave her instructions in a soft, unresonant voice: how to deal with Klein, how to find the man she wanted killed, how to return. Pierce listened attentively, though he knew he would not be carrying out her orders. At some point he would have to overpower her, with or without Anita's help, make his way to Government House in Farallon City, and then do whatever his Briefing impelled.

"Ma'am, it'd sure be easier if you'd come with me into Klein's place."

"Oh, no. I'm an old operator—I don't get caught in a place where there's folks with no bracelets. Anyhow, you're a big boy. You don't need no help."

"Whatever you say, ma'am."

"Goddamn right. Now, be a good boy and get that lazy nigger Dallow off his black ass. Sun's damn near up—gotta get these people's breakfast."

Pierce rapped on the door, and Dallow was up at once, bellowing at the others. Yawning and scratching, they stumbled out into the morning mist and shaped up in two lines. Dallow called roll, turned to Mrs. Curtice, and said: "All present, ma'am."

"Okay. Get the bus cleaned up and send a detail out for breakfast. After chow everybody gets the morning off. Bring that Jap-nigger girl over here."

Dallow gestured to Anita, who followed him. Pierce turned to go with them.

"She din't say nothin' about you. Git in that bus and help stow the bedding."

Reluctantly, Pierce obeyed, but he stayed close to the open door. It wasn't hard, with his sharpened hearing, to eavesdrop.

"You know what your friend is gonna do today?"

"Yes."

"Show respect!"

"Yes, ma'am."

"Well, you better hope he does it, 'cause if he screws up—or goes AWOL—I'm gonna mess you up. Know what it feels like to have one of these bracelets round your neck? You don't ever want to find that out, honey. So you make sure he knows what you're in for. Understand me?"

"Yes, Mrs. Curtice . . . You're in pain."

"So what?"

Pierce stepped into the doorway; he could see Mrs. Curtice sitting on the bench, with Anita and Dallow facing her at the usual distance.

"I can take away the pain."

"Is that right."

Then Pierce saw blank astonishment in Mrs. Curtice's face. She gasped and stood erect.

"Oh my God! Oh—my—God! What you—what—what you done to me?"

"I've blocked the pain."

"Oh my God." She took a few tentative steps. "I can walk. And it don't hurt at all." Her face showed shock, delight, and then alarm. "This is some kind of trap!"

Pierce realized, too late, what was happening, and saw Mrs. Curtice's fingers tighten on the wand. He leaped from the bus, but he was too far away to do anything. None the less, Anita might be able to take advantage of any distraction he could create. He got five or six steps toward them before the pain smashed up his arm. Everyone was screaming and falling—she had triggered all the bracelets at once.

Somehow Pierce kept his feet. His peripheral vision vanished. He was staring down a long tunnel at Mrs. Curtice, at Anita vomiting as she collapsed under the collective agony of thirty people, at Dallow springing at Mrs. Curtice, his face contorted. Dallow hit the old woman hard, knocking her flat. The wand splashed into a mud puddle.

The pain went on, and on. Pierce staggered and fell, and crawled awkwardly on one hand and his knees. Mrs. Curtice, pinned under Dallow's convulsing body, screamed in renewed pain and groped frantically for the wand.

Pierce grasped it and turned it off. Everyone in the group had been shrieking, but suddenly it was very quiet. The children sobbed.

Dallow picked himself up. Mrs. Curtice lay still, her clothes soaked in mud, her face unreadable. She looked at Pierce.

"I was right."

"About what?"

"Everything. You're a real pro, you are. Nobody but a pro could keep moving with a hot bracelet on."

"Dallow, help her up."

Dallow lifted her gently while she spat and hissed with pain, and carried her into the bus. Pierce bent over Anita, touched the pulse in her throat. Her skin was clammy with sweat. He picked her up and followed Dallow to the bus. As he did so, he heard the morning shape-ups in the other campsites, and realized no one had bothered to investigate the horrible uproar they had made.

The two women lay almost side by side in the doorway of the bus. Mrs. Curtice never took her eyes off Pierce.

"Boy, you're in real trouble now."

"Is that right," said Pierce.

"Incitement to riot. Inducing an indent to abrogate his contract." She glared at Dallow. "Theft of person-nel-management equipment. I'll have the law on you, you bastard. And your weirdo girlfriend. Hope the bitch dies. And, Dallow, you're goddamn well finished. I'll have you so fucking blacklisted you'll have to go endo or starve."

"Put a bracelet on her, Dallow."

"Hey, man, you sure? She no indent."

Pierce looked balefully at him. Dallow fished a bracelet out of his jacket and sealed it around Mrs. Curtice's bony wrist. She made no resistance.

"Bring 'em up out'a the gutter, make somethin' of 'em, see they're fed and clothed and got work—look at the th-thanks you get. Oh, Billy Dallow, how c-c-*could* you?"

"Miz Curtice—that girl, that Anita, she *healed* you. She took away you pain. And what you do? You freak out, Miz Curtice, you hurt ev'body. You think we all out to get you."

She laughed bitterly. "And I was right, right. It *was* a trap, and I'da got out of it until you jumped me."

Dallow looked at Pierce. "You better not be playin' me for a fool, man. You said some smooth words las' night, you better not be lyin'."

"Don't worry, Dallow. You did the right thing." He looked down at Anita, wondering what it felt like to suffer that much pain. "I need sedatives. Something to keep Anita asleep for a few hours."

"Hunh? Miz Curtice, she don't stand for no drugs."

"You playing *me* for a fool? You've got drugs."

Looking embarrassed, Dallow climbed past the two women and fumbled about in the bus's dark interior. He returned with a hyprospray pistol and a single pink cartridge. Pierce recognized the drug—a nonprescription sedative that would keep her out for about four hours.

"Any more of these?"

"One."

"Okay." Pierce shot the drug into Anita's thigh; she trembled and relaxed. "Put her in the bunk above the cab. Mrs. Curtice, get up."

"I can't. It hurts too much."

"Get up."

Whimpering, she obeyed. He gestured to her to climb down. Somewhat absently, Pierce observed that the others were standing in a ragged semicircle behind him, watching silently.

"You're riding up front with me," he said to her. Turning to the workers, he said: "I'm the boss for a while. I've got the wand, and I'll use it if I have to. After we get to where I'm going, you can do whatever you damn well want."

"Watchoo gonna do with Miz Curtice?" Dallow asked.

"Nothing, if she behaves. If she doesn't, I'll kill her. Okay, let's get going. Everybody in the bus."

Before getting behind the wheel, Pierce retrieved his Smith and Wesson from the glove compartment and slipped it into his jacket. Then he helped Mrs. Curtice into the cab. They drove out of the camp without incident. Mrs. Curtice sat sullenly glaring out the window, averting her face from Pierce. After a few minutes, she said: "What's all this about, anyway? What the hell you doing?"

"A job."

"A job, a job. Why pick on me? What I ever do to you? I'm just a hardworking old woman, tryin' to get along—"

"Quit blubbering. You just came down the road at the right time."

"—Gonna get me in the shit with the Copos, I always had a clean record, made my payoffs like clockwork—"

"Once we get to Farallon and I finish my job, you're

on your own. You can have your wand back and everything. I don't think there's much future in blackbirding, though. Once we get one or two matters cleaned up, we're going to shake out every Colonial government from top to bottom. People like you are going to be out of business."

"Why, you sneaky son of a bitch, you're a Trainable, ain'tcha? You work for AID."

"Mm-hm."

She laughed. "The Agency ain't gonna mess with me. I done 'em too many favors."

Pierce said nothing. He reflected that he had been too high up, too specialized to be aware of everything the Agency had been doing. He was vaguely embarrassed that the Agency should deal with blackbirders, though it was not really surprising. He remembered Wigner's remark about slavery on Beulah.

Highway 605 ran up out of the Alcatraz Valley to the lower slopes of the hills of Little Frisco. Then it turned north to the Golden Gate Pass and followed the river west across the Farallon Dunes. The road was busy: logging trucks, bracero buses, and many, many Copo cars.

"Never saw so many," Mrs. Curtice said. "For Christ's sake, drive careful. They like to shake us down every time the brakes squeak."

Pierce laughed. He had the pleasant, light-in-the-stomach feeling of being in danger of his own free will, like a hang-glider stepping off a thousand-meter cliff. In a few hours at most, Gersen would be dead, Sherlock would be stalled if not stopped, and Pierce would be on his way back to Earth with a message for Wigner, and with Anita to back it up. This time tomorrow, the Gurkhas would be in control of Mojave Verde; a month from now, the Agency and all Colonial government would be thoroughly purged. After that, he could retire—but that was a long time away.

All around them the dunes stretched green and gray and blue in the mid-morning sun. Sloughs gleamed, their surfaces rippling in the wind; the dune grass waved shimmeringly. Overhead, millions of birds stormed into the sky and sank again to their ponds and thickets: snow geese, wood ducks, grebes, passenger pigeons, mallards, pintails—so many that their cries and the thunder of their wings drowned out the wind in a strange, dispassionate jubilation.

"Why'd you dope your girlfriend?"

"None of your business."

"She's got some kinda power, don't she? Something you can't control." Mrs. Curtice studied him for a moment. "And she wouldn't like whatever it is you plan on doin'. You need her, or you'da ditched her somewheres, but first you gotta do somethin' nasty. Probably kill somebody."

"Don't you worry, ma'am. The less you know, the less they'll hurt you."

"Who?"

"The Copos, if I don't succeed."

"Lord, lord. Well, it's my own damn fault for pickin' up hitchhikers." She laughed at her own wit. Pierce laughed, too.

They entered Farallon City. The bus would attract attention in the city center, but Pierce had to risk it. From the bus to Gersen's office and back must be only a brief sortie. The downtown area stood between the western slopes of Mount Farallon and the harbor. Government House, thirty stories high, dominated the waterfront skyline. At the top was Gersen's office, no doubt heavily guarded. Pierce reviewed what he knew about the building as he drove into a parking lot two blocks away. The Copos' North American headquarters took up the first five floors; above that were various agencies and departments, with the Commissioner's staff situated on the top three floors. The building would be swarming with police; it had better be, if his plan was to work.

As soon as the bus was parked, Pierce used one of his last flechettes on Mrs. Curtice. She slumped back into her seat, eyes rolled up. Pierce opened the panel to the rear of the bus: "Dallow!"

"Yo." Dallow's lean face appeared in the opening.

"I'm locking the bus. Mrs. Curtice is out; so's Anita. You people just relax for a while. I should be back in half an hour, maybe less."

"Yeah. Hunh. What if you ain't?"

"Raise hell. Scream, shout, whatever. But not for half an hour."

"Right."

Pierce left the bus, locked it, and began walking purposefully toward Government House. A hard, clean wind, smelling of salt, gusted down the street, and he could hear surf pounding the seawall. It was nearly lunch hour, and the streets were already filling with hungry civil servants.

A driveway led down into an underground garage: AUTHORIZED PERSONNEL ONLY. Pierce strode down into the garage, past the rows of Copo cars, past the duty sergeant immersed in a newspaper, into the locker room. It was empty; the day shift had been on for almost four hours.

The lockers posed no problem; Pierce's tripled sensory-input synthesis made it easy to feel out the padlock combinations. The first locker held only civilian clothes; the second, a uniform a shade too large. Just as well; he put it on over his shirt and trousers. The hiking boots looked bad, but they would have to do. The Smith and Wesson fit snugly in the long holster.

He took the elevator to the fifteenth floor, got out, climbed a flight of stairs, took the elevator another five floors. Lunch hour was well under way, and the people in the elevator gave no more than a glance at him and the others in uniform.

At the twenty-sixth floor, Pierce went to the stairs again. He was just a little shaky with eagerness.

"Hold it."

Two plainclothesmen stood by the door to the twenty-seventh floor, their pistols aimed down the stairs at him.

"Who're you?" asked the older of the two.

"Turner. Just got in from Little St. Louis. I'm supposed to report to Mr. McGowan."

"Why you on the stairs?"

"I don't like waiting for elevators, so I ran up."

"All thirty floors?" The younger man laughed.

"Sure. Like to stay in shape." Both plainclothesmen had beer bellies. "Now can I for God's sake come up and show you guys my orders?"

"Come up slow. Keep your hands where we can see 'em."

"Right."

They were office cops, very slow. Pierce dropped them without difficulty. He took their pistols, serviceable Mallorys that scarcely showed when he tucked them inside his shirt. He would have to hurry now.

Going through the door to the twenty-seventh floor, he found himself in a typing pool, rows of desks facing a supervisor's glass-walled office. A few of the typists looked up as he walked calmly to the supervisor's door. He knocked and entered.

"Sit down, ma'am. Would you mind, uh, opaquing the wall for a minute? This is a confidential matter, I'm afraid. Thank you."

He leaned across the desk. His fingers reached out, curled around her neck, and his thumb pressed against her windpipe. She was a Latin-American of thirty or so, and she looked at him with stupefied horror.

"Where's Commissioner Gersen?"

"H-he's not here. He's not in Farallon City." Her eyes were round and focused tightly on him. "I swear, I swear."

"Where is he, then?"

"I don't know, I don't know."

He pressed hard for a moment, then relaxed.

"Uh! Oh, please! Mojave Verde. He—went down yesterday, w-w-with Mr. McGowan. Please, I—"

She got a drugged flechette. Pierce went from the office into a corridor leading to the elevators. With no target, with no objective now but escape, he shivered uncontrollably. The plainclothesmen would be coming to any minute; he had little chance of slipping unnoticed out of the building, so he might as well do it in style. Besides, it would help him take out his frustrations.

A descending elevator opened its doors. Pierce drew his pistol and shot the woman and three men inside. Down the corridor, someone gasped. Pierce lunged into the elevator, pressed the button for the mezzanine floor, and turned to study his unconscious traveling companions. All were plainclothes Copos; had they noticed his boots, he might well have been killed. He discarded the Smith and Wesson—its clip was almost empty—and replaced it in his holster with one of the Mallorys. It was fully loaded.

As he had hoped, the mezzanine was quiet. He pressed the main-floor button and stepped out. He descended a flight of stairs and found the main floor boiling with people who hurried to the elevators; the arrival of the Copos had created a useful diversion. He walked briskly outside into the sea breeze.

Damn it! How the hell was he going to get to Mojave Verde? The bus was far too slow, never mind the problems of looking after Mrs. Curtice and the indents. Then there was Anita to consider: she was quickly becoming more of a liability than an asset. Perhaps he could persuade her to go through that knotholer's I-Screen, warn Wigner personally—some such bullshit stratagem, though it seemed unlikely to work on a mind-reading genius. But he *must* get to Gersen; his Briefing would allow no one to stand in his way. If necessary, he decided, he would risk killing her; even a !Kosi was expendable when the stakes were this high.

As he entered the parking lot, he glanced at his watch: twenty-three minutes had passed. His white bracelet glinted in the sunshine. Somewhere he would have to get the damned thing removed; he detested even the potential restriction on his freedom of action. Getting into the cab, he saw Mrs. Curtice and Anita still sleeping peacefully. The panel was open; Pierce thought he'd left it closed. Dallow looked at him with a smile.

"Ev'thing smooth?"

Pierce opened his mouth to reply, but no words came. Every muscle in his body seemed paralyzed. His hands fell limply across his thighs.

Anita slid down out of the bunk onto the seat next to him. Her eyes were dark and unreadable. His jaw slack, Pierce watched her unbutton the Copo shirt, the shirt underneath, felt her push up the T-shirt and scratch her nails across his chest. Something peeled back; he felt a brief, sharp sting between his ribs.

Anita held a very small cylinder between thumb and forefinger.

"A self-destruct, Jerry. I felt the pseudoderm patch last night."

He wheezed, croaked, found he had a voice again. "That bastard."

"Who?"

"Wigner. Wigner. He's the only one who could order an involuntary implant on a Senior Field Agent. Even so, he was taking a hell of a chance. Bastard."

"Why?"

"It's not to keep me from being questioned—if it were, I'd have died yesterday morning when Shih captured me. It's an Agent abort. Once I'd killed Gersen, I was supposed to blow myself up."

"That's senseless."

"Wigner never did a senseless thing in his life." Pierce turned away, and his eyes met Dallow's.

"More trouble?" Dallow asked.

"More trouble."

"Watchoo gon' do now?"

"I don't know—we've got to get out of here. I've got to get to Mojave Verde."

"Jerry." Anita put her hand on his.

"Wigner or no Wigner, whatever Sherlock is, it's got to be stopped. I've *got* to kill Gersen. Even if I annoy my boss by living to tell about it."

"The Briefing is still running you, Jerry."

"Not much we can do about that, ma'am."

"Don't 'ma'am' me—you make me feel like Mrs. Curtice. No, there's quite a lot I can do, Jerry. I can knock you out, and keep you out for a day or two if necessary. That would at least keep you out of trouble while I tried to warn Wigner. But I don't know enough yet. You're the one with all the information."

"I'm blocked."

She took his hands in hers. "Jerry, I can Clear you. Without the drugs and machines. Without wrecking your mind."

He wanted to believe she was lying, but knew she was not. Unaccountably, he began to tremble.

"I can feel your mind, Jerry. I can feel the blocks. They're like cysts, running deep. I think I may open up some things you don't want to remember, things you're not supposed to remember, but we've got to know everything they put in your Briefing. And when it's over, you'll be your own man again. Free."

"There's no such th—" A flutter of remembrance: where, when, had he told someone that there was no such thing as freedom? What had happened next? It seemed oddly urgent, like a powerful dream not quite recalled.

"How long will it take?" he muttered.

"A few hours. Not long."

"All right. All right." He switched on the ignition. "We'd better find a quiet place to do it."

"There's a camp outta town," Dallow said. "Nobody mess witchoo there. We look after you."

Anita smiled. "Thank you, Dallow."

He smiled back. "You welcome."

The bus moved out into the traffic. Pierce drove very carefully, very slowly. He had never been so frightened in his life.

Nine:

Dallow directed them to a migrant camp a few kilometers north of Farallon, between the dunes and the sea. Pierce parked *El Emperador sin Ropa* on a site facing east, across the gray-green crests of the dunes to the snow-gleaming Coast Range. In mid-afternoon, the camp was almost deserted.

Pierce climbed out of the cab and carried Mrs. Curtice around to the back. She still slept heavily, as if her body were grateful for a respite her mind would never willingly allow. She was very light, older and frailer than she had seemed when her fingers had held the inductance wand.

After he left her, Pierce went for a restless walk around the campsite. The indents, glad to be outside at last, flopped contentedly on the sand, letting the sun soak into their bodies. Ignored by everyone, the children ran squealing around the bus and made forays down to the surf to chase sandpipers. Dallow detailed a crew to pick up a late lunch from the camp mess hall. There was an air of holiday, which Pierce did not share.

Anita came out of the bus with a couple of blankets under her arm. She spoke briefly to Dallow, who nodded respectfully. Anita turned toward Pierce.

They walked silently out of the camp, into the dunes; the wind slapped at them and drove sand like mist around their ankles. In a few minutes they were out of sight of the truck; in the lee of a dune, the air was calm. The surf thumped patiently a hundred meters away.

"This will do. Sit down, Jerry." She spread a blanket on the smooth sand.

He obeyed. She undressed and sat cross-legged, facing him. The black chromofilm was gone; her body gleamed like gold.

"I said I would Clear you, but that's not quite the word. Whatever is in your mind will stay there; it won't go into a reel of psychotape. But it'll all be accessible to you; you'll Clear yourself . . . You're very scared."

"Yes."

"With reason. Your mind is full of blocks, and I don't know which one will release your Briefing. I'm going to have to open up everything. I won't wreck your mind, but the experience will be very unpleasant. They don't put in those blocks without good reasons."

"And the whole thing'll take just a few hours?"

"Yes."

"Wouldn't Dr. Suad love to get his hands on you."

"Wouldn't he just." She smiled. "Are you ready?"

"I'm ready."

"I will feel what you feel about whatever is released, but that is all. Your memories will be your own. And when we're through, no matter what, it'll be your life, your mind, and no one else's."

"I know. I know." That was one reason he was so frightened.

"Then. . ." She closed her eyes and began to rock back and forth. A little !Kosi song whispered on the wind.

Whatever it brings, I won't look away, Pierce said to himself. Then, as he stared rigidly at the naked woman an arm's length away, he froze. The wind no longer blew; the surf had become a dull, meaningless noise. The sun blazed on Anita's shoulders, on her arms, her breasts, her thighs, but she no longer moved. He felt like a prisoner condemned for life to a single eternal quarter-second.

Then, incredibly, in that endless immobility something moved. Anita's eyes opened, her face tilted like a flower to the sun, and she seemed not just alive but afire, burning, burning bright as she walked naked into the night forest that was his mind.

He was on Ulro again. His tank had crossed the dusty bed of the East River, heading back to the Transferpoint in Queens. The early morning sun blazed through the window, throwing the cabin into dazzling contrast despite the filters.

Pierce, sweating and itchy in his spacesuit, was eager to get back through the I-Screen. It had been a good scavenge: the case in the nose of the tank was full of artifacts carefully excavated from a buried basement on Morningside Heights. Columbia University, in some form, had still existed on its old campus when Doomsday came, and Pierce hoped his cargo of broken plastic and glass would be somehow connected with whatever the university's scientists had been doing.

A TV monitor showed that his partner's tank had fallen more than a hundred meters behind. They must be back at the Transferpoint in just seventeen minutes, when the I-Screen would open for exactly three seconds.

"Trouble, Wayne?"

"Overheating a bit. No fear."

It was rough going over the beige-and-gray wasteland, since no two tanks were ever allowed to take the same route; if there were Outsiders, and they should happen to glance down at New York, they must see no sign of recent activity on the surface. They might, of course, manage to notice a tank itself, not merely its tracks, but that was a gamble the Agency had to take.

The Transferpoint was in sight now, a small flat patch in the rubble. Pierce checked the time: four minutes to go. He pressed the timed self-destruct button. After he and Wayne had lugged their cases through the Screen, their tanks would back off a few hundred meters and blow themselves to bits. Such was the caution of the scavenging teams.

"Hustle," Pierce called.

"She's goddamn well packed up on me." Wayne was two hundred meters behind now, his tank camouflaged by clinging yellow-gray dust. "Got time to pull me?"

Pierce didn't hesitate. "Sure."

He spun his tank around and roared back. By the time he reached the disabled tank, he had already computed the outcome of trying to haul Wayne's tank within jumping distance of the Screen. There would be just six seconds for them to blow their doors away, step out, grab their cases, and lurch to the spot where the Screen would appear.

"Hey, whoa," Wayne said, his voice tinny in Pierce's earphones. "Too fast."

Pierce said nothing. He slipped a hand into a remote glove, and one of the tank's tentacles snaked out and looped itself around the handle of Wayne's case. The case came out easily.

Another spin, and Pierce was racing back toward the Transferpoint.

"Jerry, you son of a bitch!"

The monitor showed Wayne leaping clumsily from his tank. The sun glared on his white suit. He ran, painfully slowly, over the treacherous surface. Pierce could compute the outcome of this decision also: he would reach the Transferpoint with both cases and a margin of thirteen seconds. Wayne would be at least forty meters away when the Screen shut down. Wayne could compute just as well, of course. And he knew perfectly well that the Screen could not be reopened until the reception cell had been thoroughly decontaminated, which would be several hours after Wayne's air was gone.

Pierce's door blew away into the blinding vacuum. He retrieved his cases and plodded slowly, carefully, over the rubble to the open patch. Wayne's breath was harsh in his earphones. He heard it as the Screen appeared, as he stepped through into the airless, lead-lined cell; when the Screen vanished, Wayne's panting cut off instantly. Another voice murmured in his phones: Wigner's.

"Good thinking, Jerry."

Air began to howl into the room, and then jets of decontamination fluid sluiced the radioactive dust of Ulro from his suit. Standing in the little room between his two cases, Pierce threw up inside his suit; the Decon squad got him out just before he would have suffocated.

The sun rose into a cloudless blue sky over the Saharan grasslands of Vala. Pierce and two rookies, a man named Cherois and a girl named Carmody, hiked across the brown prairie, a few paces behind three undersized Black adolescents. The Team had doped a hunting band last night, Tested the youths, and found these three Trainables. For some reason, Base Camp had failed to send the rendezvous helicopter, so the Team and its captives had been walking since midnight. Pierce expected to reach camp by sundown, unless the copter met them en route.

The endos, two girls and a boy, were terrified. They had wailed for a time, after the dope wore off, but Pierce's growls and gestures had kept them quiet since then. They made no attempt to escape, for which Pierce was grateful; if they did, he would have to shoot them full of dope again, and the Team would have to carry them.

He called a halt near a noisy brook. The endos all squatted to urinate, even the boy, and avoided looking at their captors. They were diuretic marvels, Pierce thought; they had stopped to piss every couple of kilometers. He leaned against a rock and scanned the sky, wishing the copter would arrive and spare them the rest of this tedious march.

The rookies offered candy to the endos, who refused it with averted faces. Carmody turned to Pierce.

"Not very friendly, are they?"

"They usually aren't. Stupid not to include tranquilizers in our drug kits—but nobody expects a rendezvous to be missed."

"Well, they'll be little lambs after we get them back to camp."

Pierce liked Carmody a lot. She was a tall, slender Irish girl with brains as well as Trainability; she had been sleeping with him since the mission began, and he was beginning to think she might be a long-term partner.

"Well, let's get going," he said.

"Ooooh!" Carmody gasped. She crumpled, the shaft of a spear drooping from her belly. Pierce spun around and saw a tall, one-eyed Black man less than twenty meters away, crouched in the waist-high yellow grass, his arm already drawn back to launch another spear. The endo children cried out in relief and fright.

Automatically, Pierce thumbed his rifle to Impact 10 and fired. The spearman howled and fell back, his blood vivid against his skin in the pure morning light.

Pierce and Cherois found cover and awaited any other attackers, but there were none. The children became hysterical, and Cherois's cuffs and shouts only upset them more. One of the girls finally broke away and ran to the body of the spearman; the other two followed her. They embraced the blood-streaked corpse, shrieking and sobbing.

Carmody was dying. An antishock drug kept her conscious, but she was obviously finished.

"The sky is so blue, Jerry," Carmody whispered. "The sky is so blue. The sky." She turned her head toward Pierce, her eyes bright with the elation of some ultimate, all-revealing discovery. "Look at the sky." Then she was dead, though her eyes were as bright as ever.

Cherois stood ineffectually beside the screaming children.

"What now?" he called.

"We wait for the copter."

In a scorching noon it finally appeared, the pilot waving blithely to them through the bubble. The children huddled together, eyes blank with terror. Flies had been crawling for hours over the bodies of Carmody and the endo. Pierce had to carry each child into the copter. Cherois brought in Carmody's body.

"What about the endo?" he asked.

Pierce was strapping the children down. "We don't have time to bury him. A gift to the ecosystem of the Sahara."

The copter lifted in a whirlwind of dust. The children, looking out the open door, saw the spearman's body dwindle; they began to rock back and forth, faces in their hands.

The deck of HMS *Trident* was a welter of shattered wood, broken iron, and smoldering canvas. A dozen dead men had been dragged into a tidy row along the starboard gunwale, and Pierce trod on one as he boarded the vanquished warship. A squad of Agency marines followed him, rifles at port arms. Pierce made his way to the afterdeck, where the ship's surviving officers stood in a formal cluster.

"Good day, gentlemen," Pierce said, feeling foolish in his Napoleonic admiral's uniform. His eyes stung from the tear gas.

A young officer, his face pale, stepped forward.

"Lieutenant George Dunstable, sir. I am the senior officer; Captain Wheeler is dead."

"Gerald Pierce—your servant, sir. I am acting on behalf of the French government, although I am a citizen of the International Federation."

"We deduced as much, sir, from the nature of your craft." A hundred meters to starboard, the combat hovercraft *Waltzing Matilda* rode the swell. She looked absurdly small next to the vast, smelly bulk of the *Trident*. "Your weaponry has carried the day, Admiral Pierce. It is my duty to surrender this vessel—"

"Permit me, Lieutenant Dunstable, to interrupt. I have no desire to seize your ship, sir, nor to make captives of you or your crew. In fact, I wish to see you all safely back in England as soon as possible."

"Sir, I beg your forgiveness, but I fail to understand."

"Lieutenant, my superiors wish to see the blockade of the French coast lifted forthwith, and the resumption of French maritime commerce. My superiors are not interested in local politics. I am sending you back to Plymouth with a videotape of this morning's engagement. I sincerely hope, sir, that *your* superiors will thereby understand that we are quite capable of destroying the entire British Navy in short order. In a day, sir! And we will, unless this war against Napoleon ceases at once."

"Sir, before I can do as you suggest, I must advise Admiral Fletcher. I believe his ship is presently off Le Havre—it will be some days—"

"Admiral Fletcher has already been advised by radio."

Dunstable nodded. Most civilized Beulan endos knew something of radio and television, though few had encountered them personally.

"Sir, I beg leave to make a request of you. Your surgeons are by repute the finest in the world. I would deem it an act of charity were you kind enough to minister to our men. Almost forty are wounded; not half will live to see England, unless you condescend to help."

Pierce raised his eyebrows. "Have you enough men to sail for home?"

"Yes, sir—"

"Then, sir, that is all I am concerned about. We are not in the business of nursing our opponents back to health. If you lose twenty men, thank your pigheaded Sea Lords and their pigheaded masters for it. If they are not utterly lost to reason, they will see in those bodies some measure of our sincerity. Good day, Lieutenant—gentlemen—and bon voyage."

The evening was warm and humid, full of the promise of the monsoon. In the garden of the Agency compound, Pierce and Dr. Chatterjee strolled back and forth. They had enjoyed a splendid dinner, and the servants had withdrawn.

"I understand your position, Mr. Pierce, but I am afraid I must refuse to cooperate. In fact, cooperation would destroy the Freedom Party's credibility with the masses, and you would be no better off than you are now."

"You underestimate your influence." Pierce smiled. "We are quite confident that a properly worded statement by you would reconcile ninety percent of the emigrants to their move downtime."

Dr. Chatterjee laughed, an oddly pleasant laugh in a man so serious. "The remaining ten percent are three hundred thousand people. How will you move anyone if three hundred thousand choose to resist you?"

Pierce stopped walking, and looked into Dr. Chatterjee's deep-set eyes.

"We are prepared to incur an attrition rate of substantially more than ten percent in effecting this movement."

"An attrition rate?"

"As you know, I'm sure, our projections indicate a minimum of four hundred thousand deaths above normal in the Greater Calcutta region in the next two years—from disease, civil disorders, and famine. We are quite prepared to lose that many, and more, to accomplish the move. In fact, there is a rather bloody-minded group within the Agency who would prefer a good fight. They feel we would eliminate what they call socially volatile elements."

Dr. Chatterjee began walking again. "I expected to hear some such threat. But actually to hear it is terribly upsetting."

"Actually to say it is also upsetting. There is no need for anyone to die, if only people will cooperate."

"Mr. Pierce—put yourself in our place. We are not consulted; we have no say in when or how we shall be moved; we have no assurance that we shall be safe from native diseases—or, for that matter, from the natives. Our culture is being irreparably distorted. And why? Because we are . . . unTrainable. Yet surely we have some rights, some freedoms."

"There is no such thing as freedom," murmured Pierce. "Consider this, Dr. Chatterjee. I wish to pluck this flower. If I do, my actions are determined by what I *must* do to obtain the flower. I must reach, grasp, pluck—" The small white blossom disintegrated at his touch.

"They are very delicate," Dr. Chatterjee observed.

"Then my next attempt will be still less free. I must, after all, consider the consequences of my actions, and therefore I must limit my actions. In any case, how did I come to choose to pluck a flower at all, let alone that particular one? What made me choose to discuss this subject with you? The impulses came unbidden into my mind, did they not?"

"Then you do not believe in freedom at all?"

"I do not *perceive* freedom at all. I perceive people obeying compulsion, internal or external. Freedom is something only God can enjoy—and then only if He does not care about the consequences of His actions. Which may very well be the case."

"Then, to use your own facile terms, I obey my own internal compulsion to remain here in Calcutta, on Earth; I reject your Agency's external compulsion. We shall resist this deportation with every means at our disposal." He extended his hand. "I bear you no personal ill will, Mr. Pierce. You are a likable man, for a slave. Thank you, and good night."

Pierce shook his hand. "Good-bye, Dr. Chatterjee."

As the tall, graying Indian turned to leave the garden, Pierce drew his Mallory .15 and fired. Dr. Chatterjee, knocked forward by the impact, fell heavily into a flower bed.

The Hutterite community was a cluster of barns, silos, and houses in a shallow valley. It was brutally cold, and a little snow sifted down out of the pale January sky.

Pierce had no real business being here in this minor deportation, but, having been in Calgary, he had decided to make the short helicopter flight north to witness the move. This particular Hutterite Gemein, unlike most of them, had chosen to fight deportation in the courts, and had nearly won. The Agency, alarmed, had exerted considerable influence on the Canadian Supreme Court as well as initiating a media fog on the whole case. As a punitive step, the Gemein would be shipped to a bleak, uninhabited area in central Texas on Tharmas; the other Hutterite communities had been allowed to settle together in the relatively benign climate of Durango on Vala.

The buses were drawn up in a row outside the compound, their engines rumbling. A bell clanged somewhere, and the adults slowly emerged from their meeting hall. The women wore heavy coats over their long skirts, and their bonnets were incongruously colorful. The men wore sheepskin jackets, black cowboy hats, close-trimmed beards. Many wore glasses; centuries of inbreeding had made the Hutterites nearsighted.

When the children emerged from the Klein-Schul, Pierce recalled that fertility was another inbred Hutterite quality, and one which would have made them candidates for deportation even if they had not resisted recruitment of their Trainable children. There were many children, nine or ten in the average family. They dressed like their parents, and their faces were clear and rosy in the cold air. An old woman supervised them; she had little to do, for they were quiet and well behaved.

As the adults began loading their luggage into the buses, Pierce walked over to the children. A girl of ten or eleven regarded him tranquilly.

Pierce smiled. "Guten Tag."

"Guten Tag, mein Herr." Her German was oddly accented, a fossil dialect preserved far from its sixteenth-century Bohemian homeland, but Pierce followed it well enough.

"What is your name?"

"Anna."

"That is a very pretty name. My name is Jerry."

She said nothing. The old woman watched him uneasily.

"Would you like some chocolate?" He took a candy bar from the pocket of his overcoat.

"No, thank you."

"Are you sure? It's very good."

"No, thank you. Sir, why do you hate us so?"

Pierce was taken aback. "I do not hate you, Anna. Not at all."

"Then that is even worse."

Pierce pressed the chocolate bar into her hand. She threw it away and ran to the old woman.

"Okay, folks, let's get a move on! Got a date with an I-Screen in Vancouver tomorrow morning." The move officer, a nervous fat man, began herding the people onto the buses. The children followed the old woman across the crusty snow, trampling the chocolate into brown fragments.

Pierce walked back across the snow to his waiting helicopter. "Let's get the hell out of this dump!" he barked at the pilot.

The town was called Garibaldi; it reposed at the bottom of a lush green Sicilian valley on Urthona. Its ten thousand inhabitants were mostly Radical Catholics, and the southern European states of Earth were heartily glad to be rid of them. At dawn, standing on a ridge four kilometers from the town, Pierce admired what their industry had accomplished in just six years: orchards, vineyards, whitewashed houses, kitchen gardens, an austere cathedral beginning to rise above the red-tiled roofs. It looked like an ideal example of a successful cultie settlement.

Unfortunately, Garibaldi also supplied the local separatist movement with food, money, and recruits; over a thousand guerillas were operating in Sicily and North Africa, and doing much too well. Garibaldi was to become a lesson and a warning.

Pierce turned to the major of Agency artillery who had accompanied him to this vantage point. The major was a tall, tanned Afrikaner exile, one of many who had found good careers in the Agency's service.

"Major, you may proceed."

"Very good, sir." The major muttered nasally into his ringmike; three seconds later, a dozen columns of white smoke rose into the sky from all around the town. They curved gently, then steeply, converging on the houses and shops around the cathedral.

The operation was mercifully swift. Half the town was pulverized, the other half merely ruined. More rockets fell: the orchards exploded in flames, the houses erupted and collapsed into piles of broken bricks, the cathedral vanished. Smoke and dust enveloped the ruins.

The major handed Pierce a pair of electronic binoculars that brought the town almost close enough to touch. Pierce watched a young woman stumble out of the empty doorway of her home. Her clothes were on fire and her face was destroyed; blood pulsed brightly from her throat. Hands outstretched, she shuffled a few steps into the street and fell. Her clothes continued to burn.

"Excellent binoculars," Pierce remarked as he handed them back.

"Nikon. Cost me a bloody fortune. But they're worth it. Bloody Japs are bloody clever with optics."

"Yes."

It was a quiet Tuesday morning, and Pierce sat in the study of his apartment, flicking through hundreds of pages of follow-up memos on recent operations. It was dull but necessary work, and he could at least take frequent breaks.

The computer-terminal flickerscreen moved at a preset rate of sixteen pages per second, fast but comfortable for Pierce, and he felt jolted when it paused for a moment, flashed RESTRICTED MEMORANDUM, and resumed its normal speed with the next item. Pierce halted it at once and punched back to the restricted memo. He respected security, of course, but this was something about one of his own operations; he had a right to know.

His Training was thorough and up-to-date, so it did not take him long to outwit the computer's security barriers. Five seconds after doing so, he had read and absorbed the memorandum.

Filed by an epidemiological team on Luvah, it described the flare-up and control of a nasty artificial influenza called Strain Zeta. Pierce, visiting his mother in Puerto Cortines on Luvah, had witnessed an endo raid on the little resort settlement. On his return to Earth, he had recommended the introduction of Zeta to the endo tribes of the Yucatán. That had been just over a month ago.

Zeta, a usefully plastic virus, had been tailored for use against Luvah's endos; within a week of its deployment, it had virtually eradicated all the tribes within a hundred kilometers of Puerto Cortines. Then it had mutated—as sometimes happened with artificial viruses—and seventy two hours later everyone in Puerto Cortines was dead. AID had promptly sealed off the whole peninsula, and Strain Zeta died out, a victim of its own virulence.

Pierce sat quietly for a few minutes. When he lifted his ringmike to his lips, his hand was shaking.

"Dr. Suad?"

He was lying on the water bed, screaming, out of his mind, yet somehow aware that Suad was nearby, a dark presence in the shadows.

"It is very hard, Mr. Pierce," Suad said when Pierce's voice failed at last. "We sometimes must ask you to do some terrible things—terrible things. They are all in a good cause, but it is hard to take the long view when you are so close, eh? And you must do these things without reflection, without question, as if they were second nature. It is very hard.

"So we Brief you and condition you, and when you come back we lock away the memories where they won't bother you. We even give you false memories. Where is your mother now, Mr. Pierce?"

"Dead. Dead."

"Of course not. She is suffering from chronic bronchitis and emphysema, and you have sent her to the Instituto Respiratorio in Nuevo Juárez. You have been writing to her every week for almost three months, ever since she moved from Puerto Cortines. She writes you less often, because she is so weak. But she is happy there, and the treatment she gets is excellent—excellent!"

"That's a lie, God damn you."

"Lies are only what we do not believe. You will believe me, Mr. Pierce. And when you do, you will feel very, very much better. You always do." He chuckled. "You come out of here a new man."

The injections began.

Occasionally, Pierce was aware of a little hollow among sand dunes where the sun was warm whenever the wind died down. He was holding a small, hard hand; it was comforting, but not as vivid, not as real, as the memories that burst in his mind like flares over a ravaged battlefield. He could smell the tobacco on the Afrikaner's breath, feel the deck of the *Trident* swaying under his feet, see the burning girl fall into the street.

Somewhere in the middle of the Clearing, Anita dissolved the block on his Briefing. Thickly, with a tongue that seemed swollen, he said: "That's it. Very, very interesting . . . Keep going."

Her hand tightened on his.

Then it was over. He rubbed his face while Anita dressed; her skin was covered with gooseflesh. About ninety minutes had passed. She huddled next to him, pulling a blanket around them.

"You look terrible," he muttered.

"So do you."

"Well. That was some Briefing. Wigner didn't put

everything in, but I can guess at what he left out." He paused, ordering his thoughts.

"He's got plenty of spies at the WDS. They kept him posted on Sherlock, and one of them learned that Seamus Brown figured out that the Sherlock field doesn't need precise alignment. Not if you just position it between the Sun and the Earth like a burning glass."

"Ah, ah—how could I be so stupid?"

"So Brown went to Gersen. And Gersen understood . . . Isn't that incredible? A Trainable teaming up with unTrainables like that."

"Not surprising, really. Brown saw the implications."

The implications. Pierce considered them. No solar flare would bring Doomsday to Earth. No alien invaders would pounce out of space. There was no need now for superweapons against Outsiders. On Orc and Ulro, an experiment had gone terribly wrong, and that was all. Doomsday was caused by a human act.

So the International Federation, welding all humanity into a single unit, was not needed. The Colonies were not needed; the Agency and all its expedients were not needed. Separatism was now legitimate—and practical, since Orc possessed a weapon Earth would be unable to counter for some time.

"Wigner had three motives in sending me here," Pierce said. "He knew about Sherlock in general—and what it meant—but not how far it had progressed. So he wanted that information. He also wanted me to abort it, preferably by killing Gersen. And he wanted me to die. He wanted to keep Sherlock a secret, preserve the whole Doomsday myth, even if there was only one chance in a thousand of succeeding. And if that meant blowing me up—" He shrugged. "And he knew all about my freezing, of course . . . Oh my God, my God."

"What—"

"They block us all, for one reason or another. All Agents. And it's the blocking that makes us freeze. I remember Suad saying so, a few months ago. 'Poor old

Jerry. Twenty-six memory blocks. You'll be freezing solid in less than a year, old friend.' "

"If the blocks are gone—you may never freeze again."

"Never. I'll be a working Trainable all my life. All my life." He should have felt jubilant, but somehow he did not.

Anita nestled against him, warming him. "And now?"

He shuddered. " 'What are you doing about Doomsday?' "

—The burning girl. She fell, and fell, and fell. She would fall forever, suspended on the screen of the Afrikaner's Nikon binoculars, on the screen of memory.

After a time, he finally said: "I know what to do."

Ten:

They returned to the bus. The indents were enjoying their holiday, but cautiously: they gossiped, played cards, smoked, slept—all out of sight of Mrs. Curtice, who sat in the rear door of the bus with her hands tied behind her. Dallow sat nearby, his truncheon in his lap, smoking. He glanced up at Pierce and Anita, and his eyes widened in surprise.

"Man, you been doin' some ex*treme* serious shit."

"Well put." Pierce stood in front of Mrs. Curtice. "How's your arthritis?"

"Fuck yourself, you goddamn—"

"Shut up!"

There was so much danger in his voice, so much pent-up menace, that her voice cut off in a gurgle. Her pale eyes met his for a moment, then looked away. Absently, Pierce realized he must have a very crazy air about him, and exploited it.

He leaned forward. "I've just gone for a stroll down Nostalgia Alley. You wouldn't believe the number of corpses I saw there, Mrs. Curtice. Not even you. Be careful."

"Arright, arright—no harm intended—I'm just upset, that's all, just upset."

"Mm. How's your arthritis?"

"Much better, thanks. Lots better. Couldn't hardly stand bein' tied up if I was feelin' bad."

"Good. You're going to help us do a job."

"Is that right? Uh, mind tellin' me what it is?"

"We're all going through that knothole your old friend Klein operates."

Her mouth fell open. She laughed; it was a most unpleasant noise. "He charges ten thousand a body, one way. You got that kinda money?"

"He'll do it for free."

"Uh. Uh-huh. Where we all goin'?"

"Everywhere. All twelve chronoplanes. A couple here, a couple there."

"This is crazy." She regretted the word at once. "I mean, it's hard to understand, y'know? What's all this about?"

"You'll know when you need to." Pierce looked at the Sun; it was mid-afternoon. He turned to Anita. "Give me the wand."

A little reluctantly, she obeyed. Pierce whistled, and the indents began to drift over.

"Listen up. We're going back into Little Frisco. You folks are going to do a job for us, and then each of you gets his freedom. This time tomorrow, you won't have those bracelets on."

They did not exactly throw their caps in the air. A young Sicilian, arms folded across his massive chest, asked: "What kind of job?"

"A very safe, quiet job. All you have to do is mail some computer cartridges. Then you're on your own."

"I rather stay with Mrs. Curtice," the Sicilian said, and most of the others nodded.

Pierce had half expected this reaction. He raised the wand. "We all got a good taste of this today. Anyone want more?"

They were silent. Pierce hoped he was bluffing.

"If you people want to stay with this old bitch, that's fine. But first you're going to go through a knothole, hustle your ass to a mailbox, register what you're sending, and come back with the registration."

"What if we don' come back, man?" asked a tall American Black. "What you gon' do then?"

"Your kids will stay with me."

He scanned their unexpressive faces for a few seconds, watching his remark sink in, watching mothers look at fathers, fathers look at children.

"All right? We understand one another? Okay, everyone in the bus. Let's get going."

They stopped in Farallon City en route to Little Frisco, and Pierce went into a replication shop. A cheerful Chinese boy, snapping a mouthful of Coca-Chew, sold him a blank computer cartridge and gestured to an empty console booth. Pierce inserted the cartridge, thought carefully for a long minute, and began to program. The whole thing took him fifteen minutes. He got up, handed the cartridge to the boy, and ordered two hundred copies.

"Oh, wow. Yeah, but it'll take like an hour, mister."

"I can give you twenty minutes. Get going." The boy looked distressed, but nodded.

While the cartridge was being replicated, Pierce hurriedly typed address stickers. The copies would go to laboratories, government offices, newsfiche publishers—all places plugged into a major computer network.

The boy stacked the copies in a cardboard box. "That must be some program."

"Not really—I just don't want to lose it." He paid and left, glad that Mrs. Curtice traveled with a sizable amount of cash. There was a mailbox outside. He dropped fifteen cartridges into it, addressed to destinations in Farallon, Glaciopolis, and Little St. Louis.

"What the hell is all that?" Mrs. Curtice asked when he returned to the cab. She was stowed in the bunk, still tied up.

"Don't you worry your pretty head about it, love." He winked at Anita, who replied with an uncertain smile.

The trip back across the dunes was uneventful; there seemed to be fewer Copos around. Pierce pulled into a McDonald's on the edge of Little Frisco, and sent Dallow in with a huge order. There was considerable excitement in the back of the bus over this unexpected treat. But Pierce allowed no one else out of the bus. As the afternoon turned into a golden dusk, the passengers of *El Emperador sin Ropa* munched their hamburgers and fries in the parking lot.

Pierce sat behind the wheel, watching the almost-full Moon rising above the hills of Little Frisco. He was reviewing all the steps they still had to take when a spark suddenly began to burn very brightly on the Moon.

"Look," he said to Anita, with a mouth full of french fries. Mrs. Curtice squinted through the windshield from her bunk.

"Sherlock," Anita said.

"Works like a charm. That's why Gersen went down to Mojave Verde, to watch the launch."

The spark's intensity grew as they watched. It was centered on the Sinus Medii, virtually the dead center of the Moon's face; Pierce suspected that that was no accident, but a deliberately aimed-at bull's-eye.

The Sun set; the Moon climbed into a sky made pale by that pinpoint of fire.

"It's dimming," Anita said at last.

"No, but it's reddening around the edges. Beam's ejecting white-hot material that cools once it's out of the impact area. It'll make a gorgeous crater."

"More likely a rill. The beam is moving."

She was right. The spark had begun to shift toward the Sea of Fertility. It was winking like a star now, its light distorted by the turbulent lunar atmosphere it had created out of dust and vaporized rock; it left a track of ugly red, a new cicatrix on the Moon's scarred face.

In ten minutes the beam traversed perhaps a thousand kilometers. It winked out, leaving purple afterimages; then, almost at once, it reappeared at Sinus Medii and moved due north.

"They control the field pretty well," Anita observed. "Gersen could write his initials up there if he wanted to."

"I think I know what their strategy must be. First Gersen shuts down all the I-Screens, so no one can get off Orc to report funny lights on the Moon."

"But Earth can still send people in—"

"Doesn't matter, if Orc can control who goes out.

Anyway, that's only a temporary precaution; they'll need just a day or two. Then they launch another spacecraft—and an I-Screen generator—into orbit around Orc. They turn the I-Screen on, move the spacecraft through to Earth's chronoplane, and that's it. In another day or two, the Sherlock field would be in position, aimed right at Earth. Gersen reopens Orc and gives the IF his terms—independence for Orc or Doomsday for Earth. He might even burn another crater on the Moon, just to show them he's serious."

"No," said Anita, "on Earth. He'll want everyone scared. If he blows a hole in Australia, or the Himalayas, there'll be more pressure on the IF to give in."

Pierce nodded. "Well. We don't have much time, but I think we can screw Gersen—*and* Wigner. Finish your hamburger."

They drove several blocks in silence before Mrs. Curtice cleared her throat.

"You people *both* Trainables?"

"Yes," said Pierce.

"Is that right. And you act just like ordinary folks. What the hell do Trainables need with a bunch of broke-down indents?"

"Not much. Just a few hours' work."

"Illegal, ain't it?"

"Extremely."

"Well, I don't mind that, but don't you get my people into nothin' dangerous."

"Not a chance, Mrs. Curtice. No danger at all." In Greek, he asked Anita: "Are your powers weak?"

"Yes, but not gone."

"When we speak with the—" he groped for the Greek equivalent—"the gatekeeper, can you make him feel comfortable and trusting?"

"Yes, unless he is seriously disturbed or alarmed."

"Good." In English again: "Mrs. Curtice, you're coming in with us to see Klein."

"You gonna tell him we're all goin' through for free?"

"Yes."

"Wouldn't miss that scene for the world."

Their destination was a shabby two-story factory, not far from the Transferpoint: KLEIN & SON STORAGE CELLS. A good front for an operation that demanded heavy, regular use of electricity. Pierce parked in the factory's lot, next to a loading dock; no one was in sight, but there were lights on inside. He slid back the partition: "Dallow. We'll be back out in a few minutes. Anybody gives you trouble, hit 'em."

"Hm!" Dallow nodded and grinned.

Moving unhurriedly, Pierce and the two women got out of the bus and walked inside. A dusty corridor, its sides lined with cardboard boxes, led to a small office where a young man sat with his sandaled feet on a desktop. A radio murmured a news story about influenza spreading on other chronoplanes, and the impending closing of all I-Screen traffic. The young man, listening intently, held a finger to his lips until the item was over.

"Hi, Mrs. Curtice—good to see ya. Sir—ma'am. Sorry to make you folks wait. Some story, huh? They say it could be the worst flu since '06. My ma died in that one."

"Remember it well, Tim. Thought your dad would never get over it. Rest her soul. Well, they close the Screens, you and your dad'll make a pile."

"About time, too. It's really been slow lately."

"Your dad in?"

"Sure is. Right through the door."

Pierce was relieved at the ease of entry. Mrs. Curtice had supplied him with passwords to use with Tim Klein and his father, Horst, but her presence alone was enough to get them in. They went through the door into a small anteroom whose echoes indicated armor plate in the walls. A loudspeaker buzzed:

"That you, Herman?" A password.

"It's not the milkman," Mrs. Curtice responded.

The door to Klein's office slid open; they entered an office as neutral and impersonal as the first one. Klein, a short, stocky man of fifty, sat at a desk facing them. Pierce was fairly confident that there was a gun trained on them.

Klein studied them for a moment, then asked: "Mrs. Curtice. What can I do for you folks?"

"These two are phonies," Mrs. Curtice said conversationally.

Instantly, Pierce sprang forward and slapped Klein across his face, then shoved him away from the desk.

"Don't move," he commanded softly. Without taking his eyes off Klein, he said to Mrs. Curtice: "You treacherous old savage. I ought to kill you."

"Well—worth a try, wasn't it? Can't blame me for tryin'." She sniffed. "Fast son of a bitch, ain'tcha."

"Mr. Klein," Anita said urgently, "you're in no danger if you do as we ask, and we succeed. If we fail—if the Copos find us—they'll massacre all of us, just to make sure no one talks."

"That's *your* story," Mrs. Curtice growled.

Klein's face was pale; his thick cheeks trembled with anger. "Wh-what is this all about?"

"It's all right, Mr. Klein." Anita stepped forward, put a comforting hand on his arm. "We're friends. We're not going to hurt you."

The knotholer visibly began to relax. "This is a dangerous business, you know. We have to be so careful."

"That's over now. All the worries, all the fear, over. You and your son will be safe." Her words were just background music; the real message, Pierce knew, was going through Anita's fingers into Klein's arm.

"What do you want?"

"Eleven round trips, one to each chronoplane. Tonight."

"Oh, that's very dangerous. Too much power drain. The authorities will notice, and then I am out of business."

"By the time they can notice and react, it won't matter," Anita murmured.

Pierce watched Klein's transformation with interest. After years of living under stress, Klein was almost collapsing with gratitude for the tranquility Anita gave him.

"Whoever you are, you are not phonies. I will help."

"Thank you," Anita said.

Relaxed or not, Klein was now all business. "I must work out a schedule. How long are the trips to be?"

While Mrs. Curtice, disappointed, sat scowling in a chair, the others concentrated on logistical details. After a time, she interrupted:

"You people are gonna screw up everything, you know that? I don't know what you're doin', but it's gonna mean the end of everything. I can just feel it." Her distress was real.

Pierce looked at her. "Everything is ended anyway, Mrs. Curtice. The IF—the Agency—it's all over. That spark on the Moon was the end. All we're trying to do is to keep Gersen from using it on Earth." He smiled without amusement. "When this situation is resolved, I'm sure you'll be able to go back to blackbirding. If that's any consolation."

The preparations were soon finished. Pierce returned to the bus and climbed in the back. The indents regarded him balefully; one of the children whimpered.

"We're ready," he told them. "I'm going to send you inside in pairs. You listen to the man and do exactly what he tells you. Each pair will take fifteen cartridges through the I-Screen. On the other side you'll mail them, registered. Then you come back and jump through the Screen when it goes on. You go AWOL, or you don't bring back the registration tabs, and the kids will pay for it."

"What if we get picked up by the police over there?" asked the young Sicilian.

"That'll be too damn bad for the kids. So don't get picked up. No matter what chronoplane you go to, you won't be more than a kilometer from a mailbox. Okay, let's go. You—and you."

He escorted them, two at a time, into the building, down the corridors to the I-Screen. It was an old machine, salvaged from some university after the IF declared I-Screens a government monopoly. But it would work as well as any official Screen.

Still, it was a slow business. After each pair went through the two-meter Screen, Klein and his son had to recalibrate for the next chronoplane. Pierce prowled restlessly between the bus and the building, fingering the wand. He stood in the dark parking lot, listening to the anxious chatter of the remaining indents, the whining and wailing of their children. The night air was cold, and the sky was clear. The L-shaped scar on the Moon still glowed a sullen red-orange.

The cartridges must already be in the mail on Luvah. Some would be reaching their destinations within an hour or two. Not all would be run at once, but some would, and all it would take was one per chronoplane. Earth was the only one that really mattered, but the mailings would ensure that no Colony remained ignorant of Sherlock, even for a few days.

At 2:30 A.M., the last indent pair had left and Klein calibrated for Earth. The large, low-ceilinged room was quiet. Mrs. Curtice slept snoring on a battered old couch; Pierce had decided not to use her. Anita, her eyes red with exhaustion, sat next to Klein, keeping him calm and alert.

"The kids are all asleep in the bus," Pierce told her. "Dallow's baby-sitting until their folks start coming back."

"Good."

"Here's the wand."

She accepted it distastefully. "I won't use it," she whispered.

"Neither will I—least of all on kids. But to these people you're nothing without it."

"Speak for yourself." She found the energy for a wry, conspiratorial wink. "You're as bad as Wigner."

"Mm-hm."

"Ready," Klein called. Pierce automatically patted his pockets, making sure he had the cartridges.

The I-Screen formed in a free-standing ring in the middle of the room. On most chronoplanes, the knothole opened onto wilderness or farmland, with the nearest settlement huddled around the Transferpoint a couple of kilometers north. When it opened onto Earth, however, it revealed a large, oak-paneled room and another jumble of I-Screen equipment. Pierce strode through into an overheated atmosphere dense with cigarette smoke. The Screen winked out behind him with a gust of wind.

"Hold it right there."

Pierce obeyed.

"That you, Herman?"

Pierce sighed. "It sure isn't the milkman."

"Okay, turn around." Sitting behind a control console was a hard-faced man in a green turtleneck jumpsuit. He regarded Pierce with calm wariness.

"What's your story?"

"I'm doing a round trip; I'll be back in half an hour."

The knotholer laughed. "Hell of an expensive trip."

"You have no idea. How do I get out of here?"

"Up those stairs behind you, and out the door. When you come back, knock three-one-two. Got that? Thr—"

"Got it, got it." He was already on his way.

The door was a fire exit leading to an alley. It was early evening, with a damp February chill. The low hum of traffic resonated like a hive, and the sidewalks were thick with people. Pierce walked quickly, looking for a mailbox. He found one, fed the cartridges one by one into the registration slot, tore off the receipts, and walked away again. Signs everywhere asked:

WHAT ARE YOU DOING ABOUT DOOMSDAY?

He felt an unaccountable mix of emotions about the men and women who surrounded him: liking and regret, fondness and guilt. Each of them, happy or not, successful or not, pursued some private destiny that Pierce had just changed. Some, who might have lived long, would die young because of what he had done;

others would be reprieved. (A stroboscopic memory: the Roman camp in the snow, the general and his catamite dying surprised. This was what Pierce knew best, the toppling of empires. His own would make a very loud crash.) Please don't be too angry, he asked the crowds. I think I'm doing what you'd want me to do—what you'd do yourselves.

He entered a corner drugstore, went to the phone booths, and plugged in his ringmike. He punched Wigner's home number in New York, and the unhuman voice of the computer whined in his ear: "Four dollars for the first three minutes, please." He slid his credit card into the slot, knowing it would enable the Agency to trace him pretty quickly. "Thank you."

Wigner's phone rang twice before his answerer, in a voice almost identical to the computer's, said: "Please code."

"Pierce. Piggly Wiggly." Absurd password games. Everyone watched too many spy shows—especially the spies.

"Thank you." A click, then another ring.

"Hi, Jerry."

"Hi, Eric. The balloon's going up. They tested Sherlock a few hours ago on Orc. Burned a couple of big grooves on the Moon. They'll probably put a magnetic lens into Earth space within forty eight hours."

"Good work."

"Mine or theirs?"

Wigner laughed.

Pierce went on: "I hear Gersen's shut down the Transferpoints, but I assume you're sending people to Orc through our own Screens."

"Not yet. We've had some foul-ups."

"Mojave Verde. That's the important spot. And Farallon City. Get the Gurkhas in as fast as possible."

"Will do. Where are you, Jerry?"

"In San Francisco, as you must know perfectly well. Not for long, though."

"Come on home then, Jerry me lad." That was a

code phrase, designed to trigger a Briefing Pierce no longer obeyed. He laughed.

"Not a chance, Eric. I'm off to spread the good news about Doomsday."

"Spread—" Wigner paused, for once at a loss. When he spoke again, his voice was cold with rage. "You must be mad. Think of the consequences."

"I have."

"Command, Jerry: I bid you good day."

Feeling a little giddy, Pierce put his lips closer to the ringmike and said: *"Bang!* Arrgghh. Oh, they got me, Sheriff. I'm a goner. Ride on without me, fellas."

"Command, Jerry! I bid you good day!"

"I heard you the first time. That's supposed to make me self-destruct, isn't it, Eric? Too bad. I've been disarmed, so to speak. See you in a day or two. And get those goddamn Gurkhas into Mojave Verde." He hung up, feeling not giddy but desolated: Wigner tried to kill me. Directly, in person. Wigner.

He left the drugstore and walked back to the alley. The people on the sidewalks seemed foreign to him now; their faces were opaque, unreadable. Whatever he might do to save them, he did not understand them, did not belong to them or with them. How could they have allowed their lives to be directed by men like Wigner—or like himself? What criminal laziness or cowardice or apathy possessed them?

Well, he had the consolations of his craft, and his old boyish pleasure in making things go smash.

"That didn't take long," said the man in the green jumpsuit. "You still got twelve minutes."

"I'm efficient."

"Ha. Or *she* was. Like a cup of tea?"

"Sure."

"Earl Grey. Very nice stuff." He waved Pierce into a hanging-basket chair near the I-Screen ring. "You're the first round-tripper in—gee, almost a year. Mostly we get rich Backsliders. They make a pile downtime, but they're too dumb to stay there and enjoy it. So they pay us a fortune, and pay the forgers even more for phony papers, just to live in some uptime dump full of rats. Burns my ass to see 'em. Christ, I'd love to get downtime, start a vineyard on Los."

"Well, why don't you?"

"Oh, I will one of these days, soon as I make enough to get started properly. No point in going downtime to a joe-job. Trouble is, I got a wife who doesn't want to leave. She says this is where the action is." He shrugged. "Sure, action. So what? You got the right idea, bud. Come uptime for business, then back down again."

"Mmm." Pierce enjoyed his tea in slow, careful sips, then looked at his watch. "Want some really good advice?"

"Sure."

"Get the hell out of here. Right now."

The man's face tightened with suspicion. "What for?"

"In about fifteen minutes the whole city will be crawling with Agency gorillas. They're sure to find this place. You better be a long way away."

"Shit. What did you goddamn well do, anyways?"

"Got a computer terminal at home?"

"Sure. Built right into the cinevision. So what?"

"Watch the terminal. You should see what I did before noon tomorrow."

The man looked perplexed. "How is it going to show up on the terminal?"

"I wouldn't want to ruin the surprise." He stood in front of the I-Screen. "No kidding—get out of here. By this time tomorrow, the heat should be off, but if they nail you before then, they'll take you to pieces and stuff you down the garburator."

The man looked a little sick. The I-Screen blinked on; Pierce waved and stepped through.

Klein smiled. "Last out, first back. Now we start pulling back the rest."

"Right."

"Mr. Pierce—we are making very heavy demands

on power. If they investigate too soon, what do we do?"

"It won't happen. They'll have other things on their minds."

"Confidence becomes you," Anita said. "Now, will you please tell me how those cartridges are going to tie up the Copos?"

Pierce laughed, an oddly mischievous guffaw. "Where's your computer terminal?" he asked Klein.

"My office."

"Good. That's where Anita and I will be for the next while. I'll order in some food."

Over the next two hours Pierce and Anita ate a late supper, talked with the returning indents, and watched the glowing blue screen of Klein's terminal. Not long before dawn, Pierce dozed off; a minute later, Anita shook him awake.

"Look."

The screen was pulsing red; white letters crawled across it.

CODE JJ 16 VIOLET PRIME /PRIORITY XII
EMERGENCY OVERRIDE EMERGENCY OVERRIDE EMER-
GENCY OVERRIDE
ALL STATIONS SUSPEND NORMAL OPERATIONS 2 HRS
FROM RECEIPT
REPEAT FOLLOWING MESSAGE FOR 2 HRS
NO FURTHER OVERRIDES PERMITTED FOR 2 HRS

The letters faded, replaced by a succinct description of Sherlock and its implications. The whole message took some four minutes to creep across the screen, then repeated.

"You've preempted the whole computer network," Anita said.

Pierce nodded. "It was harder than it looks—the cartridge had to go through several test commands before it would override. And even that couldn't happen until some trusting soul put the cartridge into his terminal. But it means that every terminal hooked into this network is carrying the message. It can't be overlooked or suppressed."

Anita began laughing. "What a wicked man! Think of all those innocent housepersons who won't be able to make breakfast because the computer won't talk about anything but Sherlock."

"Tragic. But this won't do much good unless Wigner gets his troops to Mojave Verde. If the Sherlock missile manages to get into Earth space, this little message will just help to soften people up. The awful Colonials with the death ray."

"What's the problem?"

"I spoke with Wigner. He mentioned foul-ups. Once I'd have taken that as stalling. Now I suspect he's really less organized than he looks."

Dallow came in. "Ev'body's back. And hungry."

"Phone up the nearest café and order some breakfast. After they eat, they can take off if they want to."

"Aw, thass too bad. This the best job we had in a long time."

Pierce and Anita were alone again in the little office, watching the letters crawl yet again across the screen.

"He tried to kill me. Wigner. Right over the phone."

Anita's eyes widened.

"Oh, don't look so outraged. Eric's all right; from his point of view, he feels he's doing the right thing. And what I'm doing is a threat to everything he stands for."

"You're very forgiving of a man who's treated you like a—a utensil."

"He's the closest thing I've got to a friend, Anita. You don't let go of a friend just because he does something stupid or cruel."

"What a strange man you are."

"Mm."

Pierce found a portable cinevision plate in Klein's desk and turned it on. UnTrainable broadcasting always bored him, but it was worth putting up with this morning. A slightly haggard young woman was reading the news:

"—still tying up all computer networks. Trading has been suspended on the Glaciopolis Stock Exchange, and government offices have been paralyzed. Hospitals report several fatalities caused by the computer override as patients failed to receive automated therapy and medication.

"It's still not clear whether Commissioner Gersen will respond personally to the charges made against him in the mysterious message still displaying on all terminals. A Government House spokesperson in Farallon City says Gersen is in Moiave Verde and isn't expected to return until tomorrow night. The spokesperson denied that the Commissioner's tour of the Missile Facility is in any way related to the so-called Sherlock Project, which was reportedly suspended several weeks ago.

"The same government source says Sherlock was certainly not the cause of the unusual lunar light observed yesterday. No explanation has yet been offered for *that*, but some scientists speculate that an anti-matter meteor may have collided with the Moon.

"In other news, the I-Screens are still closed as the new flu strain continues to spread from one chronoplane to the next. Government health officials say the quarantine will remain in effect until a vaccine is developed; that may not be for another week. But there's no cause for alarm. No cases of the so-called Tharmas B flu have been reported anywhere on Orc."

She chanted her way through the rest of the news, ignored.

"If he's not due back till tomorrow night," Anita said, "It's because the Sherlock missile is due to be launched before then."

Pierce reviewed what he knew of Mojave Verde's launch capabilities. "Maybe as early as tonight; more likely tomorrow morning. They won't want to foul up the countdown. If Wigner doesn't get there in time—"

"You want to go south?"

"I don't *want* to, but we can't take a chance, not if Wigner is having trouble getting mobilized."

"How will you get there in time?"

"Oh—something dramatic, like renting a car from Hertz-Avis. Want to come with me?"

"I'd get in your way."

"We make a good team."

"Not in this case. I'm exhausted—couldn't do a thing. And you'll probably have to hurt people. Go alone."

He shrugged and stood up. "I'm going to see if Dallow found breakfast. And I want to get those damn bracelets off everyone."

"Good—that's something I'll be glad to help you with."

The indents sat in little clusters around the empty ring of the I-Screen; they smoked, slept, compared trips. Tim Klein, the knotholer's son, blearily drank coffee in an armchair while his father slept on the floor by the couch, where Mrs. Curtice also slept. Dallow was nowhere in sight.

"Got some good wirecutters?" Pierce asked; after some rummaging, Tim retrieved a thermocutter from a tool chest. Pierce nodded his thanks and began with the young Sicilian, who tried to protest:

"I lose my job, I go to jail."

"A man must take his chances in this world," Pierce replied in Italian.

"And my family, sir, what of them?"

The thermocutter burned through the tough plastic. "They have endured pain and slavery on your account; could freedom be worse?" He handed the Sicilian the thermocutter. "Release your family and pass these around." He yawned, stretched, rubbed his face. His whiskers were growing back; it would be good to have his beard again.

By the time Dallow and a couple of other indents had returned with boxes of doughnuts and a styrofoam coffee urn, most of the people were free. Dallow cut himself free with an enigmatic smile.

"It spooky out there," he said. "Ev'body walk

aroun' lookin' stoned. Nobody talk to nobody. Ex-
treme."

"They'll get over it," Pierce said. He could imagine
the streets of towns on a dozen chronoplanes, filled
with people whose lives had been brusquely overturned
by the crawling letters on the terminals. Some had been
jolted right out of life altogether: they had gone to join
the burning girl and Dr. Chatterjee and all others be-
nevolently murdered. At least, Pierce thought, they
would not suffer the final indignity of oblivion: he
would remember his victims now, he would allow himself to be haunted. It seemed a small enough penance.

Now everyone had been cut free. Klein and Mrs.
Curtice were awake, sleepily drinking coffee. The indents laughed nervously, comparing the paleness of
wrists, waiting for someone to tell them what to do.
Pierce stood up. Gradually the others fell silent.

"You did well. Because of what you did, there won't
be a Doomsday. And there won't be colonies any
more, unless people want to have them. Soon you'll be
able to go back home to Earth, or anywhere else you
like. You can be independent, or you can find a patron
again." He glanced at Mrs. Curtice, who gave him an
evil wink.

"I'm sorry I threatened your children. I would never
have harmed them. I hope they will never be
threatened again."

Their blank expressions unsettled him a bit. Just as
well; at least they weren't sucking up to him as their
new patrón.

"Anita and I are leaving now. What's left of Mrs.
Curtice's money is in the bus. Take it—you all earned
it. Then disappear for a few days. And if Mrs. Curtice
complains, she'll go to jail, not you."

"That'll be the day," the old woman muttered.

There was an awkward, pleasant moment when everyone insisted on shaking their hands and wishing them
luck. At last they left the room through the corridor to
the parking lot.

"What now?" Anita asked.

"You go to ground in some motel. I rent a car—or a plane. With a plane I could be in Mojave Verde in four or five hours."

They emerged into a cold, misty morning. Although the lot was screened from the street by other buildings, the traffic noise was loud. They were walking past the bus when there was a sudden change in the light, and Pierce saw the reflection of an oily rainbow shimmering on the bus's windshield. A gust of warm air swirled against their backs—

"*Drop!*" Pierce shouted.

He was already rolling under the bus, groping for the Mallory, as flechettes cracked and spattered on the asphalt. He caught a glimpse of their attacker striding through an I-Screen that vanished in an instant: a man with a Mallory .15 like Pierce's, a man in denim with a bolo tie glinting prettily at his throat.

Philon Richardson. The Dorian Climber, full of smiling hostility in the elevator to Wigner's floor. Sent through a portable I-Screen to zap a bad guy in the finest Agency style.

Pierce crawled swiftly under *El Emperador sin Ropa;* his heightened hearing tracked Philon's footsteps. The Dorian was moving around the edge of the lot, on Pierce's left, seeking a vantage point from which to drive Pierce into the open—or to kill him where he lay.

Twenty meters across the lot from the bus's rear, two dumpsters stood open, awaiting more garbage. They were the only effective cover nearby, but Pierce had little chance of reaching them. If Philon did—and he would—he would be able to spray flechettes under the bus.

The underside of the bus was filthy, caked with an oily mixture of mud, grease, and rust. When he reached the gas tank, Pierce scraped off some of the crust: the metal was rotten-orange with corrosion. He fired one shot into the tank at maximum impact; it punched through almost soundlessly. Gasoline squirted out, pooling aromatically between the rear wheels. Philon was almost to the dumpsters now.

Pierce crawled backward, groping for a wire. He found it, pulled, felt the insulation crumble, saw the bare wire spark.

The gasoline vapor ignited softly but emphatically into a little fiery puddle that spread and brightened. Pierce pushed himself backward, eyes stinging, out from under the front bumper.

The bus blew up, sheltering Pierce with its own bulk. Flames lashed out like tentacles through a cloud of greasy smoke; the bus settled as its rear tires exploded. Pierce sprang onto the hood, onto the cab; the rear of the bus was a curtain of fire. Crouching a little, Pierce climbed onto the roof of the bus and sprinted into the flames.

Philon was sprawled behind the left-hand dumpster, watching to see from which side of the bus Pierce would emerge. He glanced up, startled, to see a blazing figure standing in the black smoke that boiled around the roof of the bus. Pierce put three flechettes into Philon's face. Then he leaped from the bus and rolled across the asphalt until his burning clothes only smoldered. He smelled the stink of his singed hair, felt the skin tighten on his burned hands.

"I chose, you lucky bastard," Pierce panted. "I *chose!* Low impact, and I could've blown you to bits. I *chose!*"

Coughing, he lifted Philon in a fireman's carry, turned, and headed for the entrance to the factory. He saw Dallow and Tim Klein carrying Anita inside. They left an erratic trail of bright blood that glittered in the light of the flames.

"Oh—oh, Anita—"

The weight of the poor, stupid boy on his shoulders was almost unendurable. He staggered down the corridor, his feet slipping in Anita's blood.

They took her into the I-Screen room, and lowered her gently onto the couch where Mrs. Curtice had slept. The indents pressed curiously around her.

"Get away!" He dumped Philon to the floor and slashed through the clustered bodies, while one quiet part of his mind asked: What's the hurry? She's dead, she's dead.

She was dead, her body ripped open by the fusillade meant for him. Her golden skin was already dull, her blood already dark; her open eyes gazed thoughtfully on nothingness. She was dead for no reason but chance timing, because she stood next to Pierce at the moment when Philon, reflexes hyped at least as high as Pierce's, came through the Screen knowing only that Pierce was nearby, and then saw his quarry directly in front of him.

His mother sprawled on the sidewalk, Carmody dying on the sand, the burning girl—he could not protect them, he could not save them, they were swept away from him out of space, out of time, leaving only memories that blurred and faded and cruelly sharpened. He could not save them, he was the agent of their destruction, and he was mad enough to try to save the world.

With difficulty, he made himself stop gasping for breath. Sirens were sounding outside.

"Everybody out!" Klein bellowed. "This way!"

The indents followed him without confusion; an Algerian woman helped Mrs. Curtice, who limped past Pierce without a glance. Nor did Pierce waste time on her; he turned, stopped, and rifled Philon's pockets.

Good: credit cards, passport, other documents, all in the name of J. Nathan Swift—one of Wigner's little jokes, no doubt. The photos of Philon did not at all resemble Pierce, but no one looked closely at IDs.

He also found a little locket on a fine gold chain. Pierce recognized it: the locket he had given Judy a few days ago, the locket he had brought back from the Philadelphia goldsmith on Beulah.

Unhurriedly, despite the stink of smoke and the approaching sirens, Pierce pulled off his blackened clothes and dressed himself in Philon's embroidered denims. They were not to his taste, but they would do.

He rubbed a hand over his head: his hair had not been too badly singed.

Philon was coming to as his hyped metabolism burned away the drug. Pierce turned the Dorian onto his belly, planted a knee between Philon's shoulder blades, and twisted his fingers into the cord of the bolo tie. Philon gasped. His limbs were still to numb to move.

"What did you do to Judy?"

"She—she was a stooge for the separatists. Fed 'em information. Wigner realized it after the cat's-paw nearly got you."

"Gersen wanted me to come to Orc—why would he try to kill me?"

"Wasn't Gersen. A cell of Trainables on Earth, friends of Judy's. They didn't know anything—thought they were doing Gersen a favor if they could get rid of you."

"So you executed her."

"I was ordered to."

"And what brings *you* after me, old friend?"

Philon said nothing. Pierce twisted the bolo cord hard, then loosened it.

"You went rogue. That's all I was Briefed on. Go to Orc, nail you, go south to Mojave Verde."

"Ahh. How?"

"Agency safe house on Chavez Street—160. A car to Farallon airport and a jet from there."

"Gee, I could listen to you for hours."

"I'm talking for my life, Mr. Pierce."

"You're lucky to have the chance. Wigner built a bomb into me." He pulled Philon's head up so the Dorian could see the body on the couch. "Know who that is, Philon? Know who you zapped?"

"I can't see her face."

"Anita !Kosi, Philon. Anita !Kosi."

"Oh no, oh—Mr. Pierce, what the hell was *she* doing here?"

Pierce curled his fingers around Philon's throat, feeling the hard, fragile lump of his larynx, the vulnerable vertebrae. Philon's face grew pale except for the three little red wounds where the flechettes had hit.

Reluctantly, Pierce loosened his grip. Once he would have performed an execution like this quickly, efficiently, with a mild pleasure and no reflection. Now he had to choose; he was a free man. But he had not expected freedom to mean suppressing his desire for Philon's death. No wonder the indents feared freedom, if it meant a constant battle between mind and reflex.

He gripped the Dorian by his hair and slammed his head against the linoleum floor. Philon's eyes rolled up. Pierce tucked the Mallory, its clip still half full, into his shirt. He walked slowly out the door that the others had fled through.

He did not look back at Anita's body on the couch. He could not bear to.

Eleven:

The corridor from the I-Screen room led eventually to an empty, unpaved alley on the far side of the building from the burning bus. The indents and the knotholers had vanished. He was alone.

For a moment Pierce felt a kind of serene detachment. No one owned him; no one had any claims upon him; he was obliged to no one but himself. If he chose, he could walk into the nearest bar and drink himself stupid, or rent a cubicle in a pornotheque, or go for a long walk out into the Alcatraz Valley—anything. The Sherlock missile might go up, or it might not; the Gurkhas might arrive in time, or they might not. He could try to interfere, but he did not need to.

—An illusion, of course; the illusion of stillness at the peak of a trajectory. He walked out of the alley, into a street full of mid-morning traffic. Many people seemed to be hurrying toward the fire behind him; others stood in quiet, intimate groups, talking softly. Pierce remembered some crisis of his childhood (Panama? Caracas? Zimbabwe?) when people had behaved like this, fearing the bombs as they hadn't feared them in twenty years. He had removed a phantom threat, only to replace it with a real one.

Chavez Street was a wooded cul-de-sac in a prosperous neighborhood; the Agency safe house was near the end, a large, low home with curtained windows. A safe house, for God's sake, in a Colony town. He rapped on the front door. A taped voice crooned: "Welcome to 160 Chavez. Please insert your ID in the slot and stand in front of the camera lens. Thank you."

Pierce complied. Philon's ID card vanished, then popped out again. The door opened: a broad-shouldered blonde in a blue leotard smiled impersonally at him.

"So you're Philon—" Her face hardened as she compared his face with the indistinct image on the video monitor. Pierce stepped forward and clipped her on the chin, caught her as she fell, and carried her into the living room.

The house was silent, even to his ears. He slapped her smartly, rousing her, and pressed the Mallory against her belly.

"It's set on ten. No bullshit. I want Philon's car and the keys to the jet."

"I don't—"

"Don't waste my time, or you'll be the Agency's very last martyr."

She surrendered, led him to a safe in the hallway, opened it, and gave him a set of keys and a passcard.

"The jet's in Hangar J at Farallon. Fuelled and ready."

He looked at the passcard. "Modified Lear 200?"

"Yes."

"Jesus Christ." The modifications included four air-to-air missiles and two .75-millimeter cannons. "Car in the garage? Good."

He took her into the nearest bedroom and knocked her out with two flechettes, then locked the door. If Philon got away from the authorities and tried to follow him, he would find little help here.

There was no trouble at the airport. His passcard showed him to be Robert R. Schneider, the registered owner of the Lear 200, which had been waiting in Hangar J for a week. After a quick checkout, he filed a flight plan to Hawaiki and took off. Twenty minutes on a south-southwest course put him out of range of Farallon's radar; he descended almost to the waves and turned southeast. Automatically, he checked out the Lear's armaments: all functioning. The plane was intended for surveillance and interdiction, usually against endos, so its firepower was not great. But it would serve Pierce's purposes, as it had been intended to serve Wigner's.

The ocean was empty, a chaos of blue and white that mirrored the sky. Here and there, the rotting corpse of an iceberg wallowed in the current, bound for extinction somewhere far to the south. Once Pierce saw a pod of blue whales, also bound south, to breed in the warm lagoons of Baja. Their great flanks gleamed in the sun; they were proud and remote, their concerns far removed from humanity's. Pierce felt a stab of envy as he passed over them, envy for their clean and simple life. Then they were gone, and he turned his attention to the coast looming ahead.

He crossed the coast not far north of Los Alamitos, and tilted the Lear into a steep climb. They would pick him up on radar, of course, but not in time to do much about it. In ten minutes he was forty kilometers above the WDS and beginning the long plunge to Mojave Verde. The Missile Facility was a small gray-brown patch of geometry against the green of the hills; from the hills to the north, smoke from fires set by Klasayat's endo hunters drifted toward the gantries.

Two fighters were climbing fast to intercept, their paths like pincers closing to crush him. Pierce got a radar lock on the northern fighter and launched one of his four missiles. Three seconds later the fighter vanished, exploded into a ball of smoke that elongated toward him like a cheated ghost.

The other pilot was more adept at evasion; he escaped two missiles and launched one of his own. Pierce forced the Lear down and away, but he was still too close when the missile detonated. The concussion flipped the Lear over; metal fragments ripped through it, and Pierce felt the controls go dead. He was falling, not diving, and the fighter pursued him like a stooping falcon.

—A ferocious jolt as Pierce ejected, and a lesser one as his parachute deployed. The fighter snarled past, began a long braking curve that would bring it back to finish Pierce off as he dropped, defenseless, to the smoke-shrouded ground.

Watching that distant, glinting dart as it arced across the sky, Pierce felt again the serenity he had known in the alley behind Klein's. He was troubled by nothing but the increasing pressure on his eardrums and the sharp stink of burning chaparral. He had tried and failed. Briefed, he had failed; Cleared, he had failed disastrously.

But there was still one chance.

The smoke thickened with a shift in the wind, and he dropped the last twenty meters through acrid grayness. The fighter pilot, losing his visual fix and overestimating Pierce's height above the ground, fired wildly and missed. The jet thundered past as Pierce hit the ground and rolled down a steep slope into the floor of a gully. Shaken, he lay unmoving for a few minutes, face pressed to the earth. The fighter's roar receded and vanished.

Slowly Pierce stood up and disentangled himself from the chute. Gathering it into a bundle, he buried it under the rocks and mud where he had fallen. But he kept the survival pack attached to the chute, and with its compass got his bearings. He had come down northwest of the Missile Facility, probably no more than twenty kilometers from Mojave Verde, and much closer than that to the endos. The wind was blowing toward the Facility; he should be able to cover much of the distance camouflaged by the smoke. Coughing, he scrambled out of the gully and began to walk.

For an hour or so the going was fairly easy, though visibility was bad; he was moving downslope through open country dotted with clumps of oak and occasional patches of pine woods.

He found the hunters where he expected to. They had heard him coming, however, and stood in a semicircle across his path. He stopped.

They were very short, thick-bodied men in shirts and trousers of deerhide. Most carried bows and arrows, a few had pistols, and one was even armed with an archaic AK-47. The rifleman stepped forward as the smoke thinned a bit. He was over a head shorter than Pierce, broad-faced and large-eyed, with geometric black tattoos across his cheeks. His thick, dark hair was tied in many thin braids.

"Greetings, Klasayat," Pierce said in the Grasslanders' purring language. "I come in brotherliness."

The rifleman recognized him, and looked surprised. "Then hawks have learned to swim, Jerry-missanan'kaa." Deathwalker—his old title.

"Greater wonders have happened, Klasayat Horsehunter."

Incongruously, Klasayat pulled a pack of cigarettes—Salems—from a pouch on his belt, and lit one with a Zippo. Pierce smiled and laughed.

"You burn the hills and still have not enough smoke. Always you were a man of marvels, O Klasayat."

"Once I was, Jerry-missanan'kaa. All the families of the Grasslanders had fed from my kills, and many a husband hoped for one of my sons. Then you came, and destroyed us. There are no women in our camp, no children."

"You made war on us."

"And what else should men do when their land is taken?"

"I bear no anger for it. You did what men should do."

"As we shall do with you."

"O Klasayat, this smoke has clouded your wits. I am not some whimpering blue-eyes to be robbed and eaten. I am the Deathwalker."

Klasayat came closer, his eyes fixed on him, the rifle pointed at Pierce's chest. "Are you? Walking alone and dirty across the hills? I have looked in the eyes of the Deathwalker before, but I do not see him now."

Pierce laughed until the smoke made him cough. "Old friend, old war-mate, I walk closer to you than you know. Do the horses not think themselves growing safe as they flee your fires and race for the cliffs? When the sloth drinks at the tar pits, does she not see her own reflection and walk gladly to her death? And here you stand, speaking with me, yet seeing nothing."

The hunters shifted uncomfortably. Klasayat puffed on his cigarette, his dark eyes moving quickly from Pierce to his companions. Pierce knew it was his attitude more than his words that had kept Klasayat from killing him outright. The little glowing ember of hope began to brighten in his mind: what he could not do with all the Agency's weaponry, he might do with a handful of wretched, homeless hunters. This was the last chance.

"Yours was the skybird that fell, slain by the other."

"It was."

"Why does the Deathwalker, defeated, come to us if not to die at my hands?"

"To give you back your land. All of it."

"After destroying us to take it away?"

"I am the Deathwalker; I do not explain."

"And how will you do this thing?" asked one of the other hunters, ignoring Klasayat's glare.

"The men who build the firetrees, the rockets, have displeased me. I go to overthrow them. When they are driven from the land, it shall be yours again."

Klasayat spat. "What joy would we have of it? We are men alone, half-men."

Again Pierce laughed, half contemptuously. "Does Klasayat tell me he can steal a rifle, tobacco, a firemaker, but not women? Will the mountain people not beg you to accept their loveliest daughters when they see you rulers of the grasslands again?"

The hunters looked at one another, and Pierce knew he had won them, knew that Klasayat had read the same message in their dark, yearning eyes. The muzzle of the AK-47 lifted; Klasayat slung it over his shoulder.

"It is well. What shall we do, Jerry-missanan'kaa?"

"We must go into the town where the rockets nest. Quickly."

"This is not easily done. We are great thieves, and

we have often stolen from the blue-eyes' houses, but always at night."

"How close can you get in daylight?"

"Within easy bowshot of the guards, on the north side of the town."

On that side of Mojave Verde, Pierce remembered, there was dense undergrowth, some wooded patches, and outcrops of bare rock, all higher than the settlement. The town itself was a compact cluster of apartment buildings, stores, and offices—a typical *akademgorodok*. The Facility buildings were southeast of the residential area; Mission Control was at the top of a low ridge overlooking the town on one side and the launching pads on the other. The airfield was ten kilometers west of the town.

From the hunters' vantage point, he should at least be able to see the Sherlock missile if it was still on the ground; if it wasn't, there would be no point in going farther. And if the Gurkhas did arrive in time after all, he would have to disappear very quietly.

—And do what? he asked himself.

—Go endo for a while. With the Grasslanders, perhaps, if I can talk them into accepting me, or with the mountain tribes in the Panamints. Do some hunting, some thinking. A lot of thinking.

"Let us go, then."

They turned and moved silently through the smoke. For about a kilometer they walked single-file over increasingly stony terrain. Abruptly, they stood on the edge of a steep-sided ravine. At the bottom, a stream pounded over rocks; halfway down the slope, four horses lay dead or crippled.

Klasayat smiled. "You bring us luck." Some of the hunters scrambled down to butcher the horses. They took the livers and tongues, and left the rest to rot.

"A waste of meat," Pierce remarked as they resumed their path.

"There are plenty of horses," Klasayat said. "Why should we not eat well when we can?"

"You speak well," Pierce replied. Why expect

economy from the hunters who were driving dozens of species to extinction? And who was he, after all, to criticize?

Both they and the wind changed direction, and they could breathe pure air again. It was a beautiful day: the sun hung in the clear April sky, and the hills were fresh with new green. They were in open forest now, moving at an easy, steady pace under good cover. The endos noted the plentiful spoor of horse, camel, and deer, and with irony praised the blue-eyes for driving tigers and wolves out of the region.

Pierce liked them. They had been the scourge of the whole Mojave once, incorrigible thieves and woman-stealers, and quick to master the weapons they stole. But they had refused to let the blue-eyes sweep them away, had taken the invaders seriously but not fatalistically, and had made a spirited fight of it. To have lost as terribly as they had (Pierce had made a point of leaving the women's and children's corpses in their camps) and still stay alive and together was not a small achievement.

At last they crossed a wooded ridge and found themselves looking down at Mojave Verde. As Klasayat had said, the guards were very close. Fifty meters downslope, a high barbed-wire fence ran east and west. Beyond it was a strip of bare earth perhaps three hundred meters wide and then the nearest buildings. A sentry patrolled inside the fence in a jeep with an armorglass dome.

Pierce looked beyond, to the gantries rising above the next ridge. And there it was, glowing in the late-afternoon sun: a tall, blunt-nosed missile, still plugged into its umbilicals but obviously almost ready for liftoff.

"What now, Jerry-missanan'kaa?"

"I must go to the big round house on the ridge. Once I am through the fence and across the empty strip, I will have no trouble. But I will need a guide through the wire, and a distraction to lure the guards away."

"And what will you do in the round house, Jerry-missanan'kaa?"

Pierce looked into Klasayat's eyes. "I will set fire to the firetree, burn it to ashes while its roots are still in earth. When that is done, those who have displeased me will be overthrown, for that is no firetree like the others that grow there. Other men are coming at my bidding; they will seize my enemies, and all will leave. Then you will possess this land again."

"When you came to us before, you promised to destroy us, and you kept your promise. Now keep this one, Jerry-missanan'kaa."

Pierce laughed softly.

The sun went down. The Grasslanders ate raw horse liver and tongue, and exchanged hunting boasts. The lights of Mojave Verde gleamed like a carpet of stars, while the missile stood like a cathedral spire in floodlit splendor. The bare strip beyond the wire was not illuminated, though darkened floodlights were spaced along the fence. At unpredictable intervals, the sentry jeep passed back and forth.

"There is a path," Klasayat murmured. "To step away from it is to die. The great lights blaze forth, and the men inside come firing their guns. Each must step in the proper place, or all will be lost."

A sensor array, clearly, had been dug into the bare strip. Total interdiction would cause false alarms and inhibit the guards; this way, they could move quickly through clear lanes.

"How is it that you know where to step, Klasayat?"

"A strange question. We have eyes, we have noses. The path is clear to us."

"Even as you see where water-root lies buried in the dry season?"

"Just so. Can you not see such things?"

"Sometimes. But tonight I will follow where your feet go."

"Good. When shall we go? All are eager."

"Not until the firetree is ready to grow. It will not be long."

If the Gurkhas got in first, though, he would be in trouble.

The hours passed. The Moon rose, and the men talked softly, uneasily, about its terrible new scar. In the town there was still some traffic, though most houses were dark.

At 2:00 A.M., the umbilicals were detached.

At 2:30, lights began to go on in many of the houses.

"It's time," Pierce said. "Let us go."

They drifted down the slope as silently as mist, paused, and watched the sentry. Once the jeep had passed, Klasayat rose and slipped through the wire; he moved with the grace and control of a ballet dancer. Pierce followed, enjoying the test of muscle and nerve.

The Moon had already passed the zenith, casting plenty of light; if the sentry returned in time, they would stand out like totem poles. Klasayat scanned the featureless gravel, took a step, then another, paused, and turned right; they were advancing into an invisible labyrinth. Pierce stepped gently into the endo's tracks, reflecting on the moronic cleverness of the defenses. They would work only if the intruder made a mistake—a dangerously complacent assumption, especially about endos whose life had equipped them all with senses like Klasayat's.

In a very short time, the entire group was across the strip and comfortably huddled in the shadows between two storage sheds, watching the jeep go past.

"Now," Pierce murmured, "attend me well, or never see the sun rise over the grasslands again. You are to take no captives, nor slay anyone, unless they attack you. Go into the wide street of many lights; break the great windows of the stores. Take loot if you wish, but no more than a man can carry when he is running for his life. Make yourselves heard and seen, then get back across the wire. Can this be done?"

"*Hai,*" the men whispered, like wind in leaves.

"Good. Klasayat will stay with me and pretend he is my captive. Now go."

They went away, so smoothly that Pierce had to look hard to follow them toward the main street four blocks away. The hunters moved from shadow to shadow, never quite visible as more than a shift in light. He felt a professional admiration: their stealth had been just as good when he was hunting them years ago. That had been a short operation only because he had quickly switched from search-and-destroy tactics to biological warfare. Typhus in a waterhole will find the stealthiest enemy.

"Give me your rifle." Pierce ordered. Klasayat looked alarmed, and gripped it more firmly. "Do not argue, Klasayat. They will not believe you a captive, and me a captor, if you still carry the rifle."

"I obey you, Jerry-missanan'kaa."

Pierce took the rifle, astonished at its weight. Where on earth could he have found such an antique—some trapper's shack? "Put your hands behind your head. Good. Now, let us go."

They walked rapidly through the empty streets, Pierce a few steps behind the endo. Glass broke musically in the distance, and the trilled war cry of the Grasslanders cut through the darkness. With almost comic suddenness, lights went on in many windows, then went out again. Pierce glimpsed anxious faces peering through curtains, heard dogs barking.

"Keep going, you endo son of a bitch!" Pierce roared in English. They were jogging down a residential street, paralleling the main street and moving away from the disturbance, toward the ridge where the Mission Control blockhouse stood.

A jeep screeched around a corner, catching them in its headlights. The driver braked hard; his voice roared from the jeep's loudspeaker.

"Halt! Identify yourselves."

"Helmut Thiess, Physicist 6, 1701 D Street, ID number 67-671-1904."

"Who's the other individual?"

Pierce snarled in exasperation. "How the hell should I know? He's an endo, for God's sake. I found him sneaking through our yard, got his gun away from him—now I'm taking him to Security."

"I'll take him. Get him over here."

"Christ, man, never mind—they're running wild just a few blocks from here! Dozens of 'em! The people down there need every guard in town."

"Bring your prisoner over here, Dr. Thiess."

"Shit," Pierce muttered. He tapped Klasayat's shoulder with the barrel of the AK-47. "Get in the back of the jeep," he whispered.

"I will die, Jerry-missanan'kaa, and my soul will wander homeless forever if I am not given to the vultures."

"Do as I say, and do not be afraid."

The Security man, an impassive young Slav, opened the rear door as they approached. Pierce shoved Klasayat into the screen rear seat; the door clicked shut. Pierce rapped on the driver's window. The guard rolled it down, and Pierce struck out with the butt of the rifle, grateful now for the rifle's weight, and hit the guard squarely across his forehead. He slumped against his seatbelt without even looking surprised.

"Ah, you are quick." Klasayat chuckled as Pierce reached through the window and unlocked the rear door. They set off again.

"Could you not use the car yourself?" asked Klasayat.

"I choose not to." A masquerade would be too dangerous: he would have to struggle into another uniform, somehow dispose of the guard, and contrive to get past other guards, who would know every one of their colleagues. Better to appear as a courageous, public-spirited citizen with a valuable prisoner.

The blockhouse was a massive cylinder, two-thirds buried in the ridge and flanked by several outbuildings. A guard, somewhat agitated, paced outside his booth at the main entrance.

"What's goin' on downtown?" he asked.

"Endo raid," Pierce replied, closing the distance between them. "I caught this one, but there must be dozens more, all over the place."

"Holy shit! Sure picked their time, didn't they, with McGowan and the Commissioner here." He surveyed Klasayat with distaste. "Well, better get this schmuck over to Headquarters."

"Where's that?"

The guard took a step or two closer, pointed down the street. Pierce swung the butt of the rifle and knocked the guard flat on his face. Shots rang out from a machine gun somewhere down in the town. Klasayat began shaking, and Pierce felt pity and admiration for him, for his courage.

"Quickly."

They sprinted across from the booth to the main entrance of the blockhouse; the entry was empty. Through a doorway and up several flights of narrow steps. At the top, another door, which opened slowly, heavily.

They walked into Mission Control.

It was a large, low-ceilinged, semicircular room filled with tall green cabinets, the Facility's computer system. Three Trainable technicians, all teenage girls, monitored the pre-launch information pouring through their flickerscreens; the only other people in the room were Bengt Gersen, Harry McGowan, and Seamus Brown, seated comfortably before a holovision image of the missile. No one had noticed the intruders.

Pierce detached the clip from Klasayat's rifle. Six rounds—enough. He snapped the clip back in and handed the AK-47 to Klasayat.

"Stay here by the door. If I tell you to shoot, shoot only the one I point to."

"These are the great ones, Jerry-missanan'kaa?"

"The greatest in this world. Do not dream of trophies."

Obviously dreaming just such a thing, Klasayat clicked his tongue.

Pierce went softly across the carpeted floor, not toward the observers but toward the technicians. Looking over their shoulders, he saw a small screen flashing out the launch countdown: 11:17; 11:16; 11:15. Close—he had cut it very fine.

"Excuse me, please," Pierce said quietly to the senior technician. She looked up in annoyance; then, seeing a stranger, her eyes widened. Pierce patted her shoulder, then reached out across the control board. He flipped the MANUAL OVERRIDE switch, then the LAUNCH button, then LAUNCH ABORT.

Dozens of video and holo screens showed the missile; when it exploded, it was like a perfectly timed fireworks display. The missile's eight million components vanished in a fireball of orange, yellow, and black, into which the nose of the missile sank with eerie slowness. Thunder echoed from loudspeakers, drowning out the shouts of the technicians and observers, but not the shrill, warbling cry of Klasayat triumphant.

The observers turned and saw Pierce walking toward them. He sat down in one of the armchairs arranged neatly in front of the holovision, which now resembled a sort of outsize fireplace. A bottle of Fundador Cognac stood open on a little table; Pierce poured himself a drink and sipped it gratefully. Gersen, McGowan, and Brown regarded him in a trance of consternation.

McGowan, his complexion an unpleasant dark pink, was the first to recover. "W-where the hell did *you* c-c-come from?"

"The north side of town. With a friend." He nodded toward the door, and they turned to see Klasayat beaming at them over his sights.

On the screen, the missile was now only a pile of glowing rubble on the launch pad, surrounded by ineffectual firefighting crews. Gersen shook his head.

"Impossible. Impossible. Another fifteen minutes and it would have been in Earth space. Our agents there would have taken over guidance; nothing could have stopped us."

"Nothing *can* stop you, Commissioner."

"What do you mean?" barked Seamus Brown, who seemed fully recovered from the shock of losing his greatest creation. He was a thin, sallow man of thirty with hard eyes and, incongruously, a red-lipped mouth like a woman's.

"It means that at the worst, you gentlemen will spend a few months in some well-furnished jail, writing your memoirs. You'll be freed as soon as Earth starts recognizing the Colonies as independent sovereign states. The new governments will demand your release, and off you'll go, heroes of national liberation."

Brown leaned forward, listening intently. Gersen and McGowan began to lose their glazed expressions.

"You were too clever. You saw what a weapon the Sherlock lens could be, but you didn't realize that the mere existence of Sherlock meant the death of the IF, of the Agency—everything you wanted to overthrow."

"You're going too fast for me, Mr. Pierce," Gersen said; he had recovered his irony as well as his composure.

"No doubt I am, Commissioner." Pierce smiled. "Look—with no Doomsday, there's no need for forced political unity, for coercion, for deportations. Separatism is inevitable. Orc will be independent within months—maybe weeks. The Agency is so rotten with incompetence and corruption, it couldn't stop you even if the IF ordered it to. And it won't, since—as I believe you know—I spread the word to every chronoplane."

"Have some more cognac, Mr. Pierce." Brown poured him a fresh drink, then glared bitterly across the table at him. "You stupid son of a bitch! Of *course* we understood what would happen! D'you think we went to all this trouble just to—to Balkanize the chronoplanes? Pierce, Pierce—we were out to *unify* them. Under *our* rule, an alliance of Trainables and unTrainables. Not a tyranny of elitists, not a government based on a monstrous false threat."

Pierce's eyebrows rose a little; he laughed inwardly at himself for having, this late in his life, underestimated the perfidy of his opponents. "Ah . . . naive of me. You'd have replaced the false threat with a real one."

"Of course!" Brown snapped. "It would've been irresponsible not to use the power we discovered. We'd have kept humanity unified, moving together, not sinking backward into so many German principalities and petty kingdoms."

"Irresponsible." Pierce felt achingly tired, and not at all in the mood for a political argument. He was about to get up when McGowan pointed to the screen.

"Christ, look at that!"

In the holovision, a little yellow spark had appeared in the distance.

"Unidentified aircraft on the radar!" one of the technicians called out.

The yellow spark grew larger, nearer; pulsed orange; vanished. A few seconds later the screens went white, blacked out, then came on again to show pad and gantry utterly demolished. There was no trace of the firefighters. Parachute flares threw a flat bluish light over the blasted launch site.

Pierce cleared his throat. "I believe the Agency has arrived at last."

Gersen cocked his head, listening to the computer murmuring in his ear. His large, bland face revealed little. He spoke into his ringmike: "Tell Deputy Minister Wigner he can meet with us here in Mission Control."

So Eric himself had come along. Pierce wondered what they would have to say to each other.

Someone switched the video screens to monitor the area in front of the blockhouse. The guard Pierce had knocked out was still lying there, a small pool of blood around his head. Approaching from the street were two or three squads of Gurkhas, Uzis slung under their arms; they looked remarkably like Klasayat's hunters. As they took up positions near the blockhouse entrance, an armored personnel carrier pulled up. Wigner, looking a bit uncomfortable in a khaki uniform without insignia, got out; three young colonels followed him. Pierce recognized them all, tough Russians with plenty of combat experience.

"There'd better be more booze than this," Pierce observed. "Wigner's friends are all serious drinkers."

"Harry," Gersen said to McGowan, "would you get out the champagne, please? And glasses." He smiled faintly at Pierce. "We were saving it to celebrate."

"Jerry-missanan'kaa, what now?" Klasayat called.

"Come and sit with us."

Klasayat joined them smiling as he settled himself gingerly into a chair. Brown and McGowan looked disgusted; Pierce realized the endo smelled pretty powerfully of smoke and raw liver and unwashed deerhide. Oblivious, Klasayat flourished his cigarette and lighter, and savored the splash of cognac Pierce gave him.

"Sit in stillness," Pierce muttered, "but be ready. I do not know what the men who come will do."

"*Hai.*"

The heavy door swung open; the three colonels strode in with Wigner in their wake. He looked more like an aging NCO than the superior of field-grade officers.

The room was very quiet except for the clump of the newcomers' boots. Pierce saw one of the colonels recognize him and turn to Wigner. Wigner saw him now, and smiled through his mustache.

"Hi, Jerry."

"Hi, Eric."

There was some fuss as more chairs were found and champagne was poured. On the holovision, the pad and gantry still burned.

"Nothing pleasanter than a drink by the fireside with good company," Wigner remarked. The colonels laughed heavily. No one else did. "I gather you beat us to the punch, Jerry."

"Mm."

"Damned resourceful. *We* very nearly didn't get downtime at all, thanks to your little computer stunt. The Federation Executive Council tried to dismiss me, just on principle."

"It would be the first time they ever did anything on principle. I'm sure you charmed them."

"Charm had nothing to do with it. I had to kick some sense into them. Took time." He sighed as he sipped his champagne. "Well, well. And what in hell has happened to you?"

"I've been Cleared, Eric. All the blocks are gone. I remember everything."

Wigner nodded. "Carmody?"

"Yes."

"Lovely girl. Too bad. She was the best thing that ever happened to you, Jerry."

"No." He felt a dull, deadly pressure growing behind his eyes. It took terrible control to keep from pouncing on Wigner, killing him. "The best thing was Anita !Kosi. Philon killed her yesterday."

Just for a moment, alarm shone in Wigner's eyes. He grimaced. "I'm very sorry. I didn't know she was—"

"You don't even know what you lost when your cat's-paw shot her, Eric. But I know what *I* lost."

Wigner hurled his glass at the holovision in sudden fury. *"Damn* you for a self-pitying moron! Don't you know what *humanity* has lost? D'you have any idea? Earth is already turning into a goddamn zoo. Riots, protests, fucking insurrections! They've burned down Paris Transferpoint. Fifteen countries screaming for immediate changes in the IF, or else. Hundreds of deaths. And the Colonies sure to start breaking away, sure to start fighting Earth and each other. Jerry, you idiot, you've thrown us back into the middle of the twentieth century."

Pierce finished his champagne. Slowly, carefully, he put his glass down.

"Eric. Eric. You chew me out, congratulate yourself, and miss the point, all in one tantrum. You think you've been doing humanity a favor, even if you've had to kill a few million people in the process. And you still think you could've gone on doing it, even after you knew Doomsday would never come—"

"If you hadn't acted independently, there was a slim

but definite chance of maintaining the status quo. Any chance at all was better than facing anarchy. We decided to take that chance."

"We? *Who* decided?"

"The Minister and the Advisory Committee."

"Who all trust you implicitly—they have to, you give them all their data. *You* decided, Eric. *You* acted independently to turn Doomsday from a mistake into a hoax, and you're so goddamned insulated from reality, you actually thought it would work." The pressure behind his eyes was building. "The Agency is a shambles, the Colonies are concentration camps with indoor plumbing. When Earth was going to pieces twenty years ago, when you and I were smart-ass kids, we looked pretty good because we kept everything propped up for a while—for a while. Ishizawa saved our asses, and we thought we had the right to go on running things."

"What if we hadn't?"

"Why, then, Eric, we'd've enjoyed the benefits of our collective wisdom, or gone under through our collective stupidity. The way we will now."

Wigner shook his head contemptuously. "You're too old for that sort of idealistic crap."

"Yeah. I'm still an eighteen-year-old, thanks to Dr. Suad. I still get a kick out of zapping bad guys."

"Well, that's one pleasure you'll be giving up." Wigner scratched himself absent-mindedly, and a short-barreled pistol appeared in his hand. "Old son, you're under arrest. So are the rest of—"

Klasayat had understood nothing, but he knew a firearm. Two rounds from the AK-47 threw Wigner back into his chair; he rebounded across the table, scattering bottles and glasses, his back spurting blood. The colonels died in the next second.

The shots seemed to ring in Pierce's ears for a long time. The technicians, somewhere far away, were crying.

"Peace, Klasayat-missanan'kaa. Peace. Your people are avenged."

"I would take trophies, Jerry-missanan'kaa."

Pierce got up slowly, aware of the gold locket in his coat. He yanked a shoulderboard from each of the dead officers. Wigner's uniform had no insignia; his unfired pistol would do.

"They are not flesh trophies," Klasayat protested.

"They are enough. Never has a man struck so high, Klasayat."

"Holy Mary," McGowan whispered. He and the others sat as if paralyzed. "How in hell's name do we get out of *this*? The bloody Gurkhas will think we put him up to it. Christ, they'll cut our balls off, they do that, you know, bloody endo's got us all in the shit—"

Pierce ignored him. He looked down at Wigner, who seemed small and slightly pathetic in death.

—I liked you a lot, Eric, he thought. You were all the friend and family I had. But what a crazy fool you were, and what a lot of harm we did together.

He lifted Wigner's hand, checked the frequency of his ringmike, and gently put the hand down again. Tuning his own mike, he spoke into it:

"Sergeant."

"Sah!" The Gurkha's voice crackled in his ear.

"This is Dr. Wigner. The prisoners will be coming out with Senior Field Agent Pierce as their guard. They're to be flown out to Farallon City at once."

"Yes, sah! Shall I detail an escort squad, sah?"

"Only to the airfield, thank you. They can use our personnel carrier. The officers and I will be inspecting this facility for the next hour or so, and I'd be grateful if we weren't disturbed, Sergeant. There's a lot of information to be studied here."

"Of course, sah. No one will disturb you. Will that be all, sah?"

"Oh—an endochronic will be coming out also. He's to be escorted to the wire and allowed to leave the area. We have no need for him."

"Very good, sah!"

Pierce turned to the others. "Keep a straight face and we'll be out of here without much trouble. Once we're in the clear, it'll just be a matter of waiting for the Agency to collapse." He explained the plan to Klasayat.

"Great is your guile, Jerry-missanan'kaa."

"Judge my guile when your feet are far away. Soon this will be your land again—I swear it, Klasayat."

"I will judge your promise when my feet are here again. It has been a great raid, Jerry-missanan'kaa, and our names will live in all the camps of the Grasslanders."

"That is something worth having, Klasayat my friend." To the others: "Ready?"

Gersen, McGowan, and Brown filed out, followed by the three technicians and Klasayat.

Their escape was anticlimactically eventless. Klasayat rode with them as far as the main gate; he bade them farewell and, smiling, patted the pouch that held his trophies. At the airfield, two of the technicians asked to stay behind with their families; the rest of the party went aboard a small, sleek Boeing 905 that had come through an I-Screen with the Agency forces.

The sky was turning from black to purple and the almost-full Moon was setting as the plane lifted from the long runway. The scar from the Sherlock beam had cooled to a dark gray; one had to search for it now.

Pierce went forward to the pilot's cabin. "There's been a change of plans," he told her. "We're to take the prisoners to Mexicopolis, not Farallon."

The pilot was a plump, motherly French-Canadian. "Okay, Mr. Pierce. We'll be there in two hours."

The Boeing turned through the paling sky. Below, just beginning to emerge from the night, the forests and grasslands of Orc stretched empty and endless.

Pierce went back into the cabin, where his companions sat in a state of mild shock. Well, it had been a rough time for everyone. Had it been only five days ago that he stepped from the Earth/Beulah shuttle and froze? Had Anita still been alive twenty four hours ago?

He sat down opposite Gersen and Brown. Brown began shaking his head and giggling unpleasantly. "What a bluff, what a bluff. Pierce, you're a genius. You fall into shit and come up smelling like a goddamn rose. You're a bastard and a nuisance, but we owe you a lot."

"Shut up."

Pierce closed his eyes, repelled by their smooth, taut faces, and listened to the soft thunder of the jets. Somewhere down there, where the thunder had already faded away, Klasayat was back among his men, making the greatest boast ever heard on the grasslands. Soon he would begin planning the restoration of his people, the marriage negotiations with the men of the mountains. Pierce did not know how to contrive to have Mojave Verde restored to the Grasslanders, but he would manage somehow. Destroyed, Klasayat had lived to triumph; his destroyer, in the same hour, felt only sorrow and exhaustion. Trainables were great ironists, but nevertheless Pierce wished he were down there with Klasayat.

Far away at the edge of the world, the sun rose over red Orc's dark wilderness and turned the plane and its passengers to gold.

Twelve:

Thirty-two thousand years downtime from Earth, Vala was nearing the end of an interstadial. The ice sheets still armored much of Europe and North America; soon they would advance again, reconquering their lost provinces.

For this reason, Vala had relatively few colonists— sixty million, perhaps. Most of them were crowded into the great cities of the tropics: Touréville, São Sebastião, Mashongi, New Carthage, Ciudad Guevara. But some settlers chose to live close to the ice, to tolerate long winters and rainy summers. Fifty thousand of them lived in Chrysopylae, on the hills where San Francisco stood on Earth.

A small, compact city, Chrysopylae lived by logging, ranching, and mining. It was separated from the tropical markets by distance and bad weather; most of its products went by I-Screen to San Francisco and other uptime centers. In this anxious year of 2020, many Chrysopylans were worried about the likelihood of a war uptime, for if San Francisco should be attacked, the local economy would collapse.

The news from Earth was ominous enough. Russia, China, and the United States were quarreling about their respective spheres of influence on several chronoplanes, including Earth itself. The New Incas, a nationalist movement led by Peruvian and Bolivian Indians, had taken Mendoza and were advancing rapidly on Buenos Aires. Indonesia had just crushed a neocommunist revolt; half a million rebels had been slaughtered, and another three million driven empty-handed through the I-Screens to Tharmas. And the International Federation, with its membership down to twenty three countries, was meeting in Geneva to dissolve itself.

Though many Chrysopylans were natives of the nations in conflict uptime, they got along well. Most were Americans and Canadians, with some Swedes and Finns and a lively community of Siberians. And there were many culties: New Luddites, Fifth Monarchists, Sokagakkai, Ishizawa's Witnesses. The mayor, now in her second term, was a Sapphist. In most respects, therefore, it was a typical backwater town.

Chrysopylae's university, however, was the largest on Vala, and one of the best on any chronoplane. Over a thousand students attended in person on its campus above the Golden Gate Pass; over a quarter million more studied by cinevision, flickerscreen, and video cassette. Less than ten years old, it already had the kind of prestige once enjoyed by Oxford and the Sorbonne.

Pierce had been on the faculty for three years now. For a year after the Sherlock affair, he had been kept under house arrest in Mexicopolis while several jurisdictions wrangled over who could try him, and for what. The IF, increasingly preoccupied by its own internal problems, failed to have him extradited; the infant Republic of Orc was in no hurry to charge the man who had rescued its first President, Bengt Gersen. At last he had been released, untried and unpunished, and had gone to court himself to sue the Republic for restoration of Mojave Verde to the Grasslanders. He had won, but Klasayat was dead by then, killed in a raid on the town Pierce had promised him. He had been too impatient.

Like most Trainable professors, Pierce had no specialty; he taught what interested him and his students. His colleagues found him reserved and impossible to involve in faculty politics. His students liked him: he had over seven hundred taking one or more of the twenty-eight courses he was teaching this semester.

They recalled that he had been involved in the big Agency scandal a few years ago, but few seemed impressed by his celebrity. There had been many scandals, many crises, since then.

It was early May, a gray noon, and snowing hard. The campus, with its steeply pitched roofs and snow-mantled quadrangles, seemed pleasantly medieval. Despite the weather, there were more people around than usual; most of them were converging on the theater building. There was to be a poetry reading today.

The theater could hold two thousand, and was almost full. Holo and cinevision cameras had been set up to record the reading; the poet's image, in two or three dimensions, would glow in the walls of thousands of homes all over the world, and like thunder, his voice would be heard somewhere on Vala at every moment for a long time to come.

The Rector of the University came out onto the bare stage, smiling broadly, and said: "Good afternoon. I have the pleasure of introducing Mr. William Blake."

Blake appeared onstage to a crash of applause. He was a stocky, prosperous-looking man of fifty-two, of medium height, in a dull-brown Beulan suit. He shook the Rector's hand, turned to the audience, and bowed. At last the applause died down.

"Thank you. Thank you. As many of you may know, I am here with an ulterior motive." He spoke with an accent that sounded remarkably like modern Bostonian. "My country, the United Republic of Great Britain, is a founding member of the Intertemporal League. The League is a free association of nations, both Futurite and endochronic; we hope your own North Valan Commonwealth, and the other sovereign states of Vala, will soon join us. Like Lord Byron, and Keats, and others, I am presently a sort of roving propagandist for the League. I do not intend, however, to belabor you with arguments on this occasion; if you wish to be belabored, you will have to watch me on the Six O'Clock News tonight." There was a ripple of laughter. "I gather I am to be interviewed by one of your local controversialists. For now, however, I would like to recite some of the poems of William Blake."

His arms spread wide; he seemed to grow larger. His blunt features glowed.

"Hear the voice of the Bard!
Who Present, Past, & Future, sees;
Whose ears have heard
The Holy Word
That walk'd among the ancient trees . . ."

That voice was a great shout, a growl, elemental as rain and fire. The words crashed out; no matter how familiar the lines, how often-heard the poet's voice, the words pounded like surf over the listeners.

The poems followed one another with scarcely a break; there was no applause. But a murmur like the wind before storm rose from the darkened seats, and Blake's voice rode on it like a soaring eagle: first a few, then more and more, hundreds were whispering the words that Blake roared out. He spoke, chanted, sang, crooned, howled: of chimneysweeps and whores, of the echoing green, of the worm in the night, of mind-forged manacles, of Urizen and Orc turning endlessly into each other, of the infinity in a grain of sand, of the eternity in an hour. With each poem more voices joined in, until Blake's was almost lost.

He stopped.

"Turn on the lights."

The lights blazed down on them, burning like haloes on the listeners' heads. People blinked, smiled tentatively at one another. An uncertain patter of applause broke out, then stopped as Blake began to sing *Jerusalem*. His strong, untrained baritone filled the hall, unaccompanied for the first three verses; for the last, all joined in.

"I will not cease from Mental Fight
Nor shall my Sword sleep in my hand

Till we have built Jerusalem
In England's green & pleasant Land."

After the reading, Pierce was among the two dozen
faculty members who lunched with the university's
guest in an unpretentious refectory. The poet who had
been so effectively dramatic on stage was quite another
man now: he was full of jokes, a first-class mimic, a
good listener. For all his Beulan traits, he was very
aware of events on other chronoplanes; when the talk
turned to politics, he was more optimistic than his
hosts.

"I have great hopes for our new League," he said.
"Already most of the nations of Beulah and Eden have
joined; Ahanian Rome is about to, and many of the
former Colonies far downtime."

"I am afraid there's little chance of our Commonwealth joining." The Rector sighed. "The government
in Habana Grande is too jealous of its new power."

"That, dear friend, is of course why I accepted your
kind invitation. And there are more of us than a handful of English poets. Look at Goethe: he has single-
handedly drawn in four German states, and the
Germanies of Earth are about to follow. Look at Jefferson, calling the Americans back to themselves. And
who is there to oppose such men but a pack of knaves
and fools?"

"I don't agree," said a professor who had a little too
much wine. "We've just won our independence; we
don't intend to throw it away. With all respect, Mr.
Blake, we don't want any more interference. We have a
right to live our own lives."

Blake laughed dangerously, a tiger of wrath encoun-
tering one of the horses of instruction.

"Our own lives. I wonder, sir, if you know how that
sounds to one whose original life was lived by someone
else. Recall that Beulah has been in touch with the Futurites for over twenty years, and no Beulan has lived
his own life since then. Least of all myself." He
paused, smiling.

"I well recall the day, long ago, when a young Futurite—disagreeable fellow he was, too—appeared unannounced in my back garden, where my wife and I were sunning ourselves. Quite naked, the two of us. Wouldn't have mattered nowadays, but then—well. The fellow was one of the first Futurites in Britain. He claimed to be a student at a university in California, of all places—named after Bishop Berkeley, of all people.

"Well, this young man claimed to be an expert in my poetry. And he presented me with a volume of my own collected verse. I was then just thirty, and had written very little, yet here was a great thick book with my name on it—and my death mask as the frontispiece."

His listeners attended him in silence.

"Most edifying, to see one's own death mask. I was delighted to see I looked quite presentable. But the poems—ah, the poems. Reading them was—mm, rather like scanning a psychotape of a dream one has had and then forgotten. I had the strange sensation of having composed the poems without having quite written them down. Though I confess some of them I could scarcely understand until I had read the critics' explications. Yet—there they were, my life's literary output, compiled, annotated, printed in millions of copies.

"I finally decided to be delighted with this event; it meant that I could turn to other projects for which I now had the time. And, after Mr. Wordsworth's lawsuit, endochronic artists were entitled to royalties from uptime publication of their works, so I found myself rather well off. My unexpected celebrity also gave me a certain influence.

"I confess I am pleased that my propaganda for the League is usually welcomed, but I am a bit—disappointed—that my poetry is too. I half-expect to be clapped in irons and transported to a penal settlement for reading such seditious matter in public. Instead I am praised, applauded, holotaped. An ironic reward for a prophet."

"Would you rather have lived and died in obscurity?" the drunken professor asked pugnaciously.

"What I would *rather* have done is beside the point, dear friend; I have had no choice. I did not ask for this position in life; it was thrust upon me by the Futurites—by powerful and frightened men, children of Urizen who feared the future so much that they destroyed the past. We have none of us lived our own lives these past twenty-two years. We have robbed ourselves and each other of the lives we might have had. Some, like me, know what those lives would have been; most can only speculate. But consider this: my precursor, the man whose poems I read and whose royalties I enjoy, died in 1827, at seventy, singing hymns at the top of his lungs. If the Intertemporal League fails, if there is war among the chronoplanes, *I* shall doubtless die much younger than that, and my last words will be: 'Which way, please, to the fallout shelter?' What consolation, then, to have seen my own death mask?"

The academics were silent for a moment; then the conversation turned to other topics. Near the end of the meal, Blake leaned across the table to Pierce.

"Are you free this afternoon, sir?"

"I am."

"Perhaps we might spend a little time in private."

"I would be honored."

When they left the refectory, the snow had stopped and the sky was beginning to clear. Blake and Pierce walked across the north edge of the campus, looking down the steep slopes to the Golden Gate Pass. Here, as on many chronoplanes, a road led through the Pass and out across the Dunes to the coast. But there was no great city under Mount Farallon here, only a fishing village.

"You made quite a bit of history around here," Blake remarked.

"That is one of the few drawbacks to living in Chrysopylae. The land here won't change much in the next twenty thousand years. The river will change its course a little, the hills won't be as bare. But it looks very much here as it does on Orc."

"Does that disturb you, sir?"

"It is hard to escape one's memories."

"We seek escape only from prisons." Blake smiled at him. "You have all time to roam in, and still the past holds you. Specters hold you."

"Yes. I'm a true child of Urizen."

They entered one of the university residences, a long two-story building. Pierce's apartment, on the first floor, was small, spare, and impersonal. He turned on the walls: the Mendocino cliffs on Ahania. The same surf broke against black rock that had broken in Judy's apartment, long ago.

"I could be donnish and offer you sherry, or would you prefer a very good vinho verde?"

"Vinho verde, by all means." Blake made himself comfortable in a rocking chair. "Thank you. Your health."

"And yours . . . I believe you have more than one ulterior motive for your visit to Chrysopylae."

"I have. You said nothing at lunch about the new League."

"I'm for it."

"Would you like to go to work for it?"

Pierce's face grew smooth and impassive. He stroked his graying beard. "What sort of work?"

"A special envoy, from the League to potential members. We very much need someone like you, Mr. Pierce. You're a Futurite who knows every chronoplane, and almost every culture. You know scores of languages. Most citizens of the League are uncouth endos like myself, or unTrainable Backsliders from Earth. We have little influence on the Futurite nations, and they are the ones who must join if the League is to survive."

"If you need diplomats, you've got Metternich."

"Bosh! The fellow's an ass."

Pierce smiled. "That is no disqualification."

"It is for us. We are serious, Mr. Pierce. You Futurites have robbed us of our proper lives. We don't propose to let you rob us of our present ones as well."

"Understood. But there are thousands of people at least as qualified as I am. Why choose me?"

"There are no schools named after those thousands. There are no statues of them in the town squares."

Pierce looked embarrassed. "If you think you can trade on my fame, I'm afraid you'll find your wallet nearly empty. My celebrity has evaporated, thank God."

"You are mistaken there, I assure you. If you ever ventured from this academic cloister, you would find yourself acclaimed everywhere you went."

"And shot at as well."

"Nonsense! You can't seriously mean that."

Pierce shrugged.

"Well, sir, what would you, then? Do you propose to remain here, peacefully teaching, until some invading army marches through the I-Screens, or a Sherlock lens turns this lovely world into another Ulro?"

Pierce stood up and took Mendocino off the walls. He plugged in another projection tape, but paused before turning it on. "You know, of course, about the new chronoplanes they've discovered far downtime, in the Permian? Four of them so far."

"Indeed I have, sir. Truly astonishing." Blake seemed perplexed by this change of subject.

"I managed to have a friend of mine hired on with one of the survey expeditions on Gondor, the nearest of the Permian chronoplanes. He was an indent when I met him, but bright; went back to school and did pretty well. He sent me this tape a few days ago."

It was a simple, homemade one-wall holoprojection with no olfaction or tactility tracks. It showed a short, lean Black man in khaki trousers and an orange parka standing on the edge of an encampment of tents and sheds. The sun was shining with a wintry brightness that made the Black man squint. When he spoke, wind blowing across the microphone fuzzed his voice.

"Hi, Jerry. Welcome to Gondwanaland Junction."

The camera panned through 360 degrees, revealing that the camp sat on the edge of a plateau above a snow-streaked valley; beyond the valley, black mountains draped in glaciers rose abruptly into a deep blue sky. An orange helicopter fluttered over the valley toward some unknown destination.

"Pretty, huh? Pretty damn cold, too. We're only four thousand kilometers from the South Pole. It's a lot nicer up north. But this valley is a rift—those mountains over there are going to be Africa, and right here is Patagonia. We have geologists screaming to get in here—they go right on screaming after they arrive. This place is ex*treme*."

The tape shifted rapidly, showing brief glimpses of the terrain and its sparse, shrubby vegetation. Dallow's voice continued, describing the scenes with the eager pedantry of the novice biologist. Then one scene appeared and held: a rocky stream bed somewhere down in the rift valley. There were still patches of snow in the shadows.

Four gigantic beasts came down the stream bed toward the camera, but too far away to be seen clearly. The camera zoomed in on them. Blake gasped and leaned forward.

"A pride of anteosaurs," Dallow's voice continued. "Aren't they beautiful?"

The beasts settled down on a sunny shelf of rock above the water. The largest was perhaps the size of a lion; it must have weighed over five hundred kilos. Its massive head was covered with blue-green scales; behind its small eyes were heavy bone ridges. Its thick neck and heavy shoulders were adorned with a mane of bright blue hair; the rest of its body was covered with shorter hair, a darker blue. It idly waved its long tail.

"That's Big Daddy," Dallow said. "The others are his harem. They must have a pretty big hunting territory, because we just r͟ ͟ı into them a few days ago. This seems to be their nesting area—they haven't left it for three days. I'm hoping we'll be able to watch them lay their eggs soon."

The females, smaller and sleeker than the male, bickered for a preferred spot alongside Big Daddy. He yawned, showing great teeth, and uttered a deep bark that echoed from the rocks. Then all four went to sleep.

The scene shifted back to Dallow at the camp. "Those are my babies, Jerry. I'm going to find out everything there is to know about 'em. And they're just one tiny bit of this world—man, there's so much to learn here, we'll be busy for a thousand years. Why don't you get yourself a leave of absence and come on down and see it for yourself?"

He grinned and waved, and the wall went blank.

Blake sat back and rubbed his hands on his trousers. "Many mansions," he said quietly.

"That's where I'm going," Pierce said. "But not on a leave of absence. For good."

"I think perhaps I understand why."

"I'm going to stand on the rocks of Gondwanaland, and sail the Tethys Sea," Pierce said as if he had not heard. He put on the tape again, advancing it to the scene of the anteosaurs and stopping it there.

"So you want to bury yourself in the past."

"It's all the present now."

"But humanity needs you, Mr. Pierce. Very much."

"Humanity needs itself. It can't rely on heroes any more. It never could."

Blake sighed, crossed his legs, and raised his glass in a reluctant salute. Smiling, Pierce lifted his own glass and drank. His eyes never left the great blue beast sprawled arrogantly on the rock, his proud head lifted to the sun.

About the Author

Crawford Kilian was born in New York in 1941. Raised in Los Angeles and Mexico City, he is a naturalized Canadian citizen living in Vancouver, British Columbia, with his wife, Alice, and daughters, Anna and Margaret. Formerly a technical writer-editor at the Lawrence Radiation Laboratory in Berkeley, he has taught English at Capilano College in North Vancouver since 1968.

His writing background includes two children's books (*Wonders Inc.* and *The Last Vikings*); critical articles on Charles Dickens and the Canadian writer James De Mille; several radio plays broadcast by the CBC; and *Go Do Some Great Thing: The Black Pioneers of British Columbia.*